The Mysterious
Shrinking House

The Mysterious Shrinking House

Original Title: *Mindy's Mysterious Miniature*

by JANE LOUISE CURRY

Illustrated by Charles Robinson

SCHOLASTIC BOOK SERVICES
NEW YORK · TORONTO · LONDON · AUCKLAND · SYDNEY · TOKYO

ISBN 0-590-03161-9

20 19 18 17 16 15 14 13 12 11 10   4 5 6 7/8

Printed in the U.S.A.   11

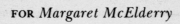

FOR *Margaret McElderry*

The Mysterious
Shrinking House

One

Mindy stood by the wide barn door and watched the two big boys carry a faded sofa out into the sunshine. Its green plush was worn almost through on the arms, and a telltale hole on one of the cushions showed that a family of mice had lived there in upholstered comfort. Mindy hoped it was an old nest or that the mice had moved out at the end of the winter, for it would be alarming to have your house suddenly lurch up and fly at a jiggle out of the sweet, musty coolness of a dark barn into a hot, glaring, fly-swarming barnyard. Mindy watched the sofa down the slope, and as the boys set it down in the crowded, sunny yard between a rusty disc harrow and an old car with a rumble seat and no wheels, she saw her mother just beyond, poking through a large carton. From the way her mother abruptly stopped poking and turned her back on the box, Mindy guessed that she had seen something special, something that would make the box worth bidding on when the auctioneer put it up for sale. You didn't dare let on beforehand that you were interested, or everyone would wander over to have a look, and someone might outbid you or fluster you into bidding more than you really wanted to spend.

The wide lawn between the barn and the yellow farmhouse was full of such boxes, along with furniture, old farm equipment, stacks of flowerpots, rolled-up snow fences, old tires, even a basket with a sweet-faced calico cat and five kittens. Mindy's father had taken one look at the kittens and at his wife and said, "*No.*" Mr. Hallam knew Mrs. Hallam's soft heart too well not to make that clear long before the auction got under way. Farm sales were great fun, and occasionally you might stumble on a real treasure. But farm sales were also dangerous—more so than Storewide Bargain Sales, for who ever came home from a bargain sale with six cupless saucers and a plate with an ugly browny-green picture of a large building with arches and columns and fancy lettering around the rim that said PANAMA-PACIFIC INTERNATIONAL EXPOSITION * SAN FRANCISCO * 1915? As Mr. Hallam pointed out, when you already have a cat-hating dog-and-a-half at home (the "and-a-half" was because it was a very large great Dane named Horace), the last thing you need is a basket of kittens. Mrs. Hallam had promised to be good. But already Mindy could see that her mother was having her usual trouble: how to keep her back turned to all of the boxes she was interested in. There were so many of them.

The boys came back. They were the auctioneer's sons, and they had been hard at work for hours, to judge from the crowded lawn. From a corner under the hayloft they brought out an old sun chair and a pair of wooden skis with broken leather footstraps. The canvas on the sun chair was faded and ripped.

"These the last?"

"Yeah. Some junk! Who's gonna pay good money for beat-up stuff like this?"

"Like Pop says, you can sell snowshoes to a goose once the bidding really gets going. Here, let's make these one lot." The older of the two tied skis and chair together with a piece of cord.

"Hoo-whee! That's it! Come on, I got the Cokes down in that little creek around the other side of the house gettin' good and cold."

They went off at a trot, the sun chair skiing between them. Down on the wide porch of the farmhouse, the auctioneer called out, "OK, folks, now you've seen it all, let's get started. Some real nice items this time. Missus Warnecki says she'd like to of taken it all to Michigan with 'em, but the old man put his foot down."

The crowd laughed comfortably. Mr. Weech said the same thing at every auction in the county, changing only the names. Everyone moved nearer the porch, and Mr. Weech's assistant carried the first carton to set it at the top of the steps.

"Aw right," Mr. Weech bawled. "Who's gonna

give us a shove off? What'm I bid for this here box of elegant crockery?"

Mindy slipped out of the sunshine and around into the cool of the empty barn. For a moment everything was a purple gloom after the glare of outdoors. She rubbed her eyes, and slowly it all came right. Yet there was a strangeness to it, something in the air besides the pleasant mustiness of old hay and vanished cows.

"Well, *nobody* likes to be empty," Mindy said aloud. The words hummed around her, and a bird fluttered among the high rafters.

The hayloft ran along above the line of empty stalls, as well as across one end of the barn. It was a peculiar arrangement and looked as if it had been made so that a hay wagon could be backed in through the wide doors for unloading, even though there was a loading door directly into the loft from outside and a clawlike hayfork rigged with rope and block and tackle under the eaves. Perhaps the barn had doubled as a coach house in the olden days, Mindy thought. It was a very old barn. Mindy's father had guessed that the farmhouse was older even than the Hallam house, which had been built in 1808.

Peering into each of the stalls in turn, Mindy saw that a little trapdoor above each manger opened down from the loft above. For putting the hay down, she guessed. Near the far wall, a rickety stair that was almost as steep as a ladder led up through a hole in the loft floor.

Mindy sneezed unexpectedly and then froze with her hand over her mouth. Above her head she heard a wild scramble of alarm—squeaks and tiny feet scurrying for cover. The sound was a little like dried peas rattling across a floor, like the squirrels on the roof at home.

Carefully, because there was no handrail, she climbed to the fifth step of the stair, from where she could see the entire loft. A small pile of straw in one corner stirred faintly. Mindy smiled and bit her lip. Mice. Maybe the ones from the old sofa. Watching quietly, almost holding her breath, her own eyes at floor level, Mindy saw a bit of straw move and, in the shadow behind it, two small, bright black eyes watching back. Mindy tried not to blink, and after a moment the mouse crept out, twitched a suspicious whisker in her direction, then abruptly made a dash for the far end of the floor above the stalls, where he whisked behind a sagging door.

Mindy scrambled to the top of the stair and followed. It was an odd place for a storeroom or a granary, if that was what the door led to. She pushed it open gingerly, not knowing what to expect. The mouse scurried out again with an indignant squeak.

"Sorry," Mindy chirped after him, with a giggle. "I'm only snooping, not mousing."

The smell was old and dry and dusty. There was no window in the tiny room, and the shadows were deep. At first it looked to be as empty as the rest of the barn. Mindy stepped in out of the doorway. By squinting, she could make out a broad plank leaning against one wall and a lumpish heap in a corner.

Nothing but a board and a pile of rubbish. Yet for some reason Mindy's heart began to thump.

"Silly! It's only trash," she said aloud, a little breathlessly. But the old barn and its silence had drawn her from the moment she had stepped out of the car. Now she had the queerest feeling that she had come to find something—something here. It was as if she had followed a string someone had left to show the way. No, it was more like being reeled in at the end of a fishline.

The board was cobwebby. Mindy turned it around gingerly with her fingertips. There, on its face, she could make out painted curlicues and lettering. The colors were faded, and one end was splintered. Once it had been an imposing sign, but now it said only:

PROFESSOR LI
MARVELOUS M

Mindy danced an excited little jig and peered around the dusty floor. She scuffled a foot through the dust and wheat chaff, but the missing part of the sign was nowhere to be found.

"Oh, grunge!"

How was she to find out what the professor professed or what it was that was marvelous? The sign lost its interest. Mindy turned to the heap in the corner and poked at it halfheartedly with her toe.

At the second nudge there was a faint tinkling crash, and Mindy saw the dim light from the outer loft reflected from glass or metal. Whatever was in the heap was swathed in a tent of dusty cobwebs,

and Mindy wrinkled her nose with distaste as she bent down for a closer look. With a piece of straw she pulled at a small hole in the cobwebbing, tearing it wider. She didn't like to touch cobwebs. They stuck and didn't want to wipe off.

It was a window. Mindy stared. A tiny window with tiny panes too filthy with grime to see through. One was broken. Mindy touched it with a hesitant finger. It *was* a window.

Frantic, Mindy ran out to the pile of straw to snatch a large handful, startling the family of mice into headlong flight in all directions. Running back, she used the straw as a whiskbroom, brushing away a wide swath of spiderweb heavy with the dust of years. She caught her breath. There just above knee level were a chimney, the gable of a pitched roof, and—under the eaves of the gable—a small round window.

"A *dollhouse!*"

Mindy ran for more straw and, forgetting her good Saturday dress, knelt in the dust to wipe away the worst of the cobwebs. Bit by bit the gray veiling pulled free, and—spiders or no spiders—Mindy picked the last strands off with her fingers. Then she leaned over and blew. In the stuffy little room the dust rose and spread around her like a thick cloud. Her sneezing made it even worse. Backing blindly through the door and groping safely to the wall, she finished sneezing in the loft. When the dust had settled, in she went again.

It was a beautiful house. Wisps of web, greasy black grime under the coating of thick dust, mouse dirt, and drifts of grain husks so ancient that they dissolved at a touch—nothing of all this could hide its beauty. Someone long ago had spent loving hours building it, for it was truly *built,* not painted plywood tacked together the way store-bought houses were. The roof was laid with tiny slates, and the walls had the look of real cut stone set with mortar. The whole was mounted on a thick slab of wood and was too heavy for Mindy to lift. She tugged at one of the handles screwed into the base but was not strong enough to pull the house more than an inch or so away from the wall.

"Oh, oh, *oh!*" Mindy flapped her hands in frustration. She felt she would burst if she couldn't see inside.

A ripple of laughter followed by Mr. Weech's delighted cackle floated thinly up to the loft.

"Sold! Sold to Miss Kathy Goble for a dollar an' two cents! Come on up an' fetch it down, honey." The high, reedy voice, faraway but clear, came through the cracks between the heavy barn siding like a voice from another world.

Sold? *Sold!* Why not? At least it was worth trying. She ran to the steps.

"A dollhouse?" Mrs. Hallam was skeptical. "It's not like George Weech and Company to overlook something like that. Are you sure? You do look a sight. What were you doing? Rolling on the floor?"

"Oh, not so *loud,* Mama. Somebody'll *hear.* Of course I'm sure it's a dollhouse. I looked." Mindy was in an agony of excitement. "Even if anybody else *did* see it back in there, they'd think it was only a pile of rubbish. Please, can we stay till the end? So's I can bid for it? They *will* sell it, won't they?" She fished in her dress pocket. "I've got . . . fifty . . . *sixty*-three cents." She frowned.

Mr. Hallam grinned. "Sixty-three cents for a dollhouse? Here, have the only nickel your mother hasn't borrowed." Solemnly he passed her a five-cent piece.

"Sixty-eight." Mindy was doubtful. "It's all grungy, but I don't know if it's *that* grungy."

"You might throw in the two cartons of empty pop bottles in the back of the station wagon," her father suggested. He slid a teasing look at his wife. "Your mother may have three or four pennies left, too, after she's bid on all her boxes."

"*And* that stack of picture frames," Mrs. Hallam added absentmindedly.

"Twelve pop bottles." Mindy took her father at his word, counting it up in her head. "It's still not even a dollar."

Her father laughed. "I can always write a check if you're that serious. I'd want to take a look at the thing, though. Dear me, and here I thought you were too old for dolls. Wasn't that what you said a Christmas or two ago?"

Mindy was indignant. "It's not the same thing at all. This isn't for *dolls*. It's a house. Sort of like a . . . a model. Besides, even grownups collect old doll furniture." She sniffed, holding back a laugh. "Even some *I* know."

Mr. Hallam, whose collection of ship models included a galleon with a captain's cabin richly furnished in the old Spanish style, nodded soberly. With the note in his voice that told her he was still teasing, he said, "Oh, *well,* if it's something of historical interest . . ."

"You'll see." She could tell he was curious.

The bidding on the cat and her kittens came to a close, and the Hallams turned their attention back to Mr. Weech. Mrs. Hallam had been outbid on one of her boxes and was ready to do serious battle for the next item, an old fruit crate loaded with metal scrap. Why, Mindy could not imagine. Still, her mother usually knew what she was doing.

The Weech boys carried the dollhouse between them awkwardly, because of its weight. As they threaded through the crowd, people drew back, wrinkling noses and hiding smiles. In the bright sunshine the house looked incredibly filthy, its lines blurred by the layered grime of many years. Even Mr. Hallam was a little dismayed.

"Ahem." Mr. Weech cleared his throat. "I have a bid of sixty-eight cents and twelve lemon soda bottles from Miss Araminta Hallam. Do I hear seventy-five cents and three cartons of bottles?"

Kathy Goble fell into a fit of giggles.

Mindy blushed at the general amusement and held her head a little higher.

"Are there any other bids? None? Gone once, gone twice . . . this lot sold to Mindy Hallam for . . . hey, Mr. Hallam? Do I hear a bid for a dozen handsome matched bottles?"

"Give you twenty-four cents, George," Mr. Hallam called.

"Done! Sold to Mindy Hallam for ninety-two cents."

People drifted away in a cheerful humor, pickup trucks and cars were loaded, and the farm road became a cloudy ribbon of yellow dust all the way out to the highway. The Hallams were last to get away, except for three teen-age boys still struggling to load the tireless Chevy coupe onto the bed of an elderly truck.

"Oh, Jack, *must* we have this dirty thing in the car?" Mrs. Hallam looked at the house doubtfully. There was barely room for it behind her own purchases.

"I have just the thing." Mr. Hallam rummaged under the back seat and came up with a newspaper and a large ragged sheet of plastic, which he spread on the open space of the station wagon floor and over the stack of frames. Then he stood back so that the Weech boys could slide the house in. He wedged it securely between the other boxes and slammed the back door.

"Don't fret, hon. It may look awful, but it doesn't stink, so it won't contaminate us." He slid behind the wheel and switched on the ignition. "Yo, Mindy. Sit down," he warned. "No hanging over the back seat. You'll get a good look soon enough."

Mrs. Hallam smiled. "She has that wide-eyed collector's look. I'm a fine one to talk, though. *I* came away with several nice things and two real treasures."

She bounced up and down a little on the seat in

her pleasure, and Mr. Hallam smiled. She and Mindy were a pair.

"Did you see the ugly speckled frame?" Mrs. Hallam asked. "There's a funny little oil painting of a corn-husking party in it, and from the clothes the farmers and their wives are wearing, I'd say it must date somewhere around 1850. I didn't dare examine it too closely for fear of showing how interested I was, but I think it may be a Linden Park! Linden Parks are *very* scarce. But even if this isn't one of his, it's a valuable primitive. Thank heavens I was the only dealer here today! No one thought the Warneckies would have anything worth bothering about, I suppose, and we knew Foxy Weech had unloaded all of his 'imported' antiques at last Saturday's sale."

"Maybe the old stuff was left by the people who lived here before," Mindy suggested. "I bet my house was, anyhow. It took a long time for it to get that gucky. But what's the other treasure?" She slid a skeptical look at the crate of broken tools and parts of lamps.

"Now, now." Mrs. Hallam grinned and turned to her husband. "I'm sorry about the junk," she said. "It can go straight into the trash barrel. But there's a pewter platter in with it that's rare as rare."

"*This* old thing?" Mindy leaned over the seat and pulled it out.

"Oh, do be careful! It's battered enough already. See those hammer marks? Those are important. And the little marks stamped on the rim? These on this side are the emblem of Henry Will."

"Henry Will?" Mr. Hallam was impressed. "He's

eighteenth century, isn't he? And what do the hammer marks mean? That it was hammered out from a flat sheet of metal instead of cast?"

"I think so. And that's very unusual in early American pewter. Mr. Henry Will was more of a perfectionist than most."

Mindy was not much interested in platters. "Do you suppose my house could be eighteenth century?" she asked.

"I hardly think so." Her mother spoke kindly. "You see, this would have been the frontier in those days, and people would be having enough trouble getting their own houses built and their land cleared to have time for making elegant dollhouses."

"That's right." Mr. Hallam agreed, but his voice held a note of puzzlement. "But you know, Nell, it does have an eighteenth-century air about it. We'll have to do some reading up on dollhouses. It just *might* be that Miss Hallam's house is the real treasure of the day." He swung the station wagon off the dirt road into the highway.

Mrs. Hallam smiled indulgently. Mr. Hallam was always spinning exciting tales to himself, seeing adventure where there was none. He and Mindy were a pair.

Two

The Hallam house was the oldest in the small mid-western Pennsylvania village of Brittlesdale: a large, handsome white-painted brick residence at the edge of the town where the highway began its climb back up into the hills. It was known to everyone in Brittlesdale as Inn House, though no one except Mrs. Bright remembered the long-ago time when it actually had been an inn. "The softest beds on the Forbes Road," early travelers had said. Mrs. Bright was a sharp-eyed, cherry-cheeked little old lady, and for as long as anyone in town could remember, she had lived in the tiny cottage up the road, just beyond the small "barn" Mr. Hallam had built at the corner of his property to serve as garage, storeroom, and workroom. Though there were only three Hallams, the house was full to overflowing because it was an antique shop as well as their home.

Mrs. Hallam managed the shop, with sound advice from Mr. Hallam and help from Mindy. Some people might not care to live in a house where even the beds and soap dishes carried price stickers and the chair you sat on today might be gone tomorrow, but Mindy liked it because living in an antique shop also meant that every little thing had a past, a story to it.

The house did, too. Mrs. Bright had told the Hallams many interesting tales about Inn House, and Mindy always remembered with delight the serious tone in which the old lady had explained that the front porch and back sun porch had never quite looked as if they belonged because, after all, they were "modern additions, you know." They had been added in 1893.

It was to the sun porch that Mindy and her father took the dollhouse. The redwood picnic table had not yet been moved outdoors for the summer, and on it they placed thick layers of newspaper and the house itself.

"Too bad we can't set it in the driveway and hose it off," Mr. Hallam observed. "But that might ruin anything inside. Let's clean off all this dust and dirt and see if we can't find the catch that opens the back. Not that I expect we'll *find* anything much inside," he added, trying manfully not to expect much.

Mrs. Hallam brought cleaning materials and several much-used plastic sponges, which Mindy proceeded to cut into fours. Mr. Hallam suggested that she use full-strength detergent cleaner on a small patch at a time, wiping the area immediately with a bit of sponge dipped in clear water. He and Mindy sat on opposite sides of the table and worked until Mrs. Hallam—after two unsuccessful attempts—made them stop and wash up for dinner.

The following afternoon—Sunday afternoon, when he usually played golf with Ed Bostweiler, a fellow teacher at Oak Ridge Union High School—Mr. Hallam worked on the house as Mindy's assistant window washer. Mindy had prepared a supply of cotton-tipped toothpicks, and they set about cleaning the film of scum from the tiny panes with ammonia water.

"The swabs are a good idea, Min." Mr. Hallam bit his lip and squinted with concentration. "But my fingers must be too big and clumsy for this kind of work. I seem to smear more than I clean."

"Oh, *oh!*"

Mindy gasped and sat back, staring.

"What is it? Cut yourself? Be careful. There's a broken pane on this side as thin and sharp as a razor blade."

"No, no. Oh, Daddy, come here and look!" Mindy whispered. "Oh, *look.*" She bit nervously at a fingernail, making room for him as he came around the table to look in the side window nearest the front of the house.

"You have to put your eye up real close," Mindy said.

What he saw was an old-fashioned parlor warmed by a fall of afternoon sunshine through a front window. Sunlight touched glass-fronted bookcases and the crystal baubles of a tiny chandelier. High-backed chairs flanked a paneled fireplace, and two matching armchairs, seats and backs plumply upholstered in what once had been a rich rust color, stood with an elegant little sewing table between them. Everything was covered with a faint powdering of dust, but because the windows had been so carefully fitted and the parlor doors inside closed—if they were workable doors at all—most of the dust and dirt had been sealed out. Had it not been for an overturned chair, a table with a broken leg, and the littered floor—Mr. Hallam guessed that the Turkey carpet was painted on—the room was so lifelike that it would hardly have been surprising had the doorknob turned and a miniature family come in to have their Sunday tea. But the tea things—plates the size of a thumbnail, shattered saucers and cups, a tarnished silver teapot—were strewn about the dusty floor.

"We've *got* to get inside," Mindy whispered. "Oh, it's wonderful, it . . . it *hurts!*"

Mrs. Hallam, drawn by the unusual silence on the back porch, was most surprised of all.

"How perfect! And that teapot! It *has* to be the real thing. A Georgian miniature! The china . . . oh, Mindy! How do we get it open?"

In the end it was Mrs. Hallam's longer fingernails that found the answer. Up under the eaves at the back of the house she happened to run a nail against a sort of trigger-catch. A crack appeared along each side about an inch from the rear corners, and with a

little careful prying, the back came off. Wall, door, and windows had been tacked and glued to a thin board that fitted into a slot in the base and could be snapped tightly to the house so that no seam showed.

There, open for what might have been the first time in fifty years or more, were two upper bedrooms, the dark front-to-back hallways, a spacious kitchen with a fireplace and a rocking chair, and a cozy little back parlor. Because several windowpanes were broken besides the upstairs one Mindy had smashed, dust and grime had been laid down thickly here. They could not find the trick to opening up the front rooms.

"At least the mice never got in," Mindy said. She pried open a tiny cupboard door. "Golly, look at the neat pots and pans! And glasses! How'll we ever clean anything so bitty? How'd they ever *make* it so little?"

Mr. Hallam stared at the stone that had come loose from a corner of the back panel, a puzzled frown on his face.

Mrs. Hallam answered slowly. "I don't know, dear. Everything here is every bit as perfect as the best doll furnishings I've seen in any museum. Oh, *Mindy!* Sixty-eight cents and two cartons of *pop* bottles!" Her laughter grew until she had to sit down to catch her breath.

On Monday afternoon Mindy ran all the way home from school. The house had been so much on her mind all day that she had muddled a perfectly straightforward question on a history quiz and flunked a surprise math test outright. In second period it had suddenly come to her that the dollhouse was not simply an exciting plaything or a perfect collector's piece. It was *too* perfect. It made no sense, but she felt a panicky wish that she had not put the newly polished pine settle from the kitchen or the marble-topped walnut washstand on a prominent shelf above the ANTIQUES sign in the front window. She had marked them NOT FOR SALE, but now repented having put them out even for show. What if the house had a long-lost owner? If the owner recognized her furniture in the Hallams' window, that would be that. She would pay Mindy ninety-two cents and take the house away. Mindy's imagination got the better of her, and she felt sure that someone —someone or something unpleasant—was looking for her house and that she had as good as put up a signpost saying THIS WAY. It became more than a feeling. For a reason she did not understand, she knew that the house was in danger; that it must not be found—not yet.

A block from home, Mindy passed old Mrs. Bright dawdling along with her shopping basket over her arm and a puzzled frown on her usually cheerful face. Mrs. Bright rarely dawdled. She usually moved with a birdlike bustle. But Mindy did not notice, for her mind was on rescuing the two miniatures from the window. She panted a "hello" and ran on.

The settle and washstand were not on the window shelf.

"Mama!" Mindy slammed through the swinging kitchen door. "Oh, Mama, they're gone! You *didn't* sell them, did you?" She dropped her books on the table.

Startled, Mrs. Hallam looked up from the carrots she was scraping without answering.

Mindy stamped. "The doll furniture I put in the window. It's *gone!*"

"Oh, that." Her mother looked relieved. "Just simmer down. They're quite safe, dear." She pointed toward the sun porch. "The house, too."

Mindy opened the inner screen door to look out.

The picnic table was covered with cartons. The largest box stood upside down where the house had been.

Over her shoulder Mrs. Hallam said, "I covered it. I haven't the foggiest notion what it's all about, but your father phoned from school this morning to tell me to put all of the cleaned furniture in the filing cabinet and lock it, and to cover the dollhouse."

"So you camouflaged it. That's neat." Mindy grinned and let out a huge sigh of relief. "Daddy must've gotten the funny feeling I got. Did you, too?"

"Funny feeling? No, at least not this morning. Your father said then he had 'discovered something,' but he wouldn't tell me over the phone. No," she said slowly, cutting chunks of carrot into the stewpot, "the 'funny feeling' came afterward." She frowned, as if puzzled at her own uneasiness.

"What d'you mean?" Mindy reached into the cookie jar.

"We-ell . . ." Mrs. Hallam made a face, as if to poke fun at herself. "There was this television repairman . . ."

"*Television* repairman?" Mindy swallowed her cookie half chewed.

"Yes. He said he had a call to come to look at our set."

"But our TV's OK. Isn't it?"

"Yes. Of course it was a mistake, but I still don't understand it. He had our name and address on his order sheet. Still, that wasn't what really bothered me." Mrs. Hallam peeled and chopped a clove of garlic as she talked. "Mr. Putt—that was his name —Mr. Putt didn't leave right away, but began to look around the shop, asking the prices of this and that. Then out of a clear blue sky, he asked . . ."

"If you had any doll furniture!" A wide-eyed Mindy spoke through a mouthful of cookie. "Oh, I *knew* I shouldn't have put those things in the window!"

Mrs. Hallam frowned at an onion. "People do occasionally ask about doll furniture, but for some reason I didn't like *his* asking."

The bell on the front door tinkled.

"Oh dear, and my hands are all garlic-and-oniony. Will you go, Min?"

Mindy brushed the crumbs from her skirt and went out through the pantry to the hallway. The bell attached to the front door still tinkled faintly, but there was no one in sight.

Mindy looked into the living room, which doubled as a part of the shop. The best old furniture was kept there, and its bookcases were full of leatherbound books and old silver. Mindy went through the room and out the other door, crossing the hall into the main part of the shop, a large room that had been the dining room when Inn House was an inn. At first it seemed as if it, too, were deserted. Mindy supposed that someone had come in, browsed a moment, and left. They had heard the bell only once, but . . .

She jumped. "Oh!"

Down behind the counter where the jewelry and silverware and unusual glass pieces were kept, a small man was calmly going through the drawers where Mrs. Hallam kept the boxed sets of silverware and items put aside for special customers.

"I'm sorry, but that's private." Mindy spoke politely but firmly. "May I help you?" She felt a small flutter of nervousness as the gentleman looked up at her blankly.

"Is it? I do beg your pardon." He spoke smoothly, but did not appear particularly sorry, and seemed in no hurry to close the drawer. His dark hair was slick and shiny, his skin had the dry and faintly yellow look of old fine parchment, and a small moustache gave him the appearance of a dapper little gentleman in an old movie. His suit was a shiny too-silky blue with a waistcoat to match, and he wore a white shirt with a thin blue stripe in it. Mindy had never seen anyone quite like him.

"I *am* sorry," he said. "But it isn't *marked* 'Private' is it?"

"Well, no," Mindy admitted grudgingly. But she did not move away.

The man slid a glance at the drawer below as he rose reluctantly. Smiling and speaking in an irritating 'aren't-you-a-grown-up-little-girl' tone, he said "You see, my dear, I am a collector of um—er glass paperweights. That may sound foolish to a pretty young thing like yourself, but as you *may* know, they are an excellent investment. I fear I do forget my manners when I come upon even a modest little collection such as this." He gestured toward the

glass-topped counter. "I thought there might be others in the drawer. So often the prize ones are tucked away." He waved his hands a little, gracefully making fun of his own enthusiasm, and smiled charmingly.

"Oh, that's all right." Mindy was relieved and a little embarrassed. A lot of customers were snoopy, especially the ones who laughed and talked about having "the antiquing bug." Besides, it was silly to think everyone was lurking around looking for a dollhouse. "Were you looking for any special kind of piece?"

"Well yes, actually." He rubbed his hands and smiled again. Almost all of his teeth showed when he smiled. "I saw your pretty little millefiori and thought you *might* have, or someone here *might* know where I could find . . ." He drew a deep breath and put a hand over his heart as if it fluttered at the very thought. "*Might* you have a *bleu de roi Clichy* overlay paperweight with a mosaic millefiori mushroom center?"

Mindy blinked. "I'll have to ask my mother. I know she has a couple of expensive ones locked up somewhere. *What* did you say it was?"

He repeated the description carefully, and Mindy went off to the kitchen, muttering it to herself so that she would not forget any of it. It was quite a mouthful for an old paperweight.

"Heavens, no!" Mrs. Hallam laughed. "Not that I wouldn't like to have one, but it's years since I've seen one anything like that. I'll wash my hands and be right with him. He might be interested in the two others I have." She was excited. "The purple one is worth at least a hundred and fifty dollars."

Mindy hurried back to the front room, puzzling how anyone could ever want a hundred-and-fifty dollar paperweight. "I bet he doesn't even weigh *papers* with them," she thought.

He was not there.

Mindy dashed to the display case. Neither the drawers nor the cases seemed to have been disturbed. The cases were always kept locked, and as a rule the drawers were, too. Mindy unhooked the key from behind a framed Victorian valentine, locking the silver drawer and checking the others. Then she hurried across the hall. No little man. The bell hadn't tinkled—she was positive this time—so he had not left.

"Mama! Mama, he's not . . ." Mindy halted beside the newel post at the bottom of the stairs, staring upward.

Mrs. Hallam hurried from the kitchen, untying her apron as she came. Mystified, she followed the direction of Mindy's stare. "Why, Mr. Putt," she gasped. "Is it you again?"

The little man stood at the head of the stairway, beaming down at them.

"I could *not* resist having a look at this handsome grandfather clock." He smiled silkily and ran a caressing finger along the case of the tall clock beside him. "And I was right! It *was* made by George Woltz of Hagerstown. A lovely old piece." He gave a charming little wave of the hand and chatted his way down to the hall and out the front door. He left Mrs. Hallam and Mindy speechless on the front porch.

"The *nerve!*" Mrs. Hallam sputtered. "*That* is Mr. Putt, the television man. Paperweights, my eye!"

Mindy glared after him as he trotted down the road to a neat blue panel truck. The sign on its side

read: L.L.PUTT—ELECTRONICS AND TELEVISION RE-
PAIR.

Mindy turned. "Mama, he was up in the den!
Could he have gotten into the file cabinet? I saw
him slip out just before he saw me and started all
that about the clock."

And the den door *was* very clearly marked PRI-
VATE.

Three

Mr. Hallam frowned as he cut himself a second slice of cake. "I don't like the sound of your Mr. Putt. This certainly seems to be our day for mysteries! There just may be a connection, if the dollhouse is as . . . um, unusual as I think."

"How do you mean?" Mindy looked up from the tiny oilcloth-covered worktable in her hand. Her father had taken it to school that morning in his attaché case. "What's so mysterious about the kitchen table?"

He frowned. "Well, first off, it's perfect. Right down to the worn patches on the oilcloth. Every blessed thing in the house is perfectly to scale."

Mrs. Hallam started, but Mindy did not see what her father was leading up to. "And so . . ." she prompted.

"Don't you see, Min? Dollhouse collections

usually have a few pieces of furniture, a picture or mirror on the wall, a candlestick or lamp—something —out of scale. Too big or too small to look quite right; perhaps bought at a different time or place. Do you know what I mean?"

Mrs. Hallam spoke thoughtfully. "You're right; and it is odd. There are the curtains, too. They're wrong."

Mindy's eyes widened. "Dollhouse curtains are always sort of stiff and bulgy. Is that what you mean?"

Her mother nodded, watching her husband as she answered. "Yes, the weave is too coarse for them to hang in the sort of folds real curtains have. But why, Jack? What are you getting at?"

Mr. Hallam took the little table from Mindy to turn it over and point to a small light patch on the dark wood of its underside. "At first I thought it might simply be that everything in the house was made by the same man. That could explain the perfect scale. But it didn't seem very likely—not all the china and glassware and metalwork, too. I took this piece into our science lab this morning because I wanted a look at the workmanship under strong magnification." He took a deep breath. "It was still perfect. Nothing that looked like tool marks, so far as I could see. On a crazy impulse I took a very thin shaving from the wood—you can see the place—and put it under the microscope."

"And? And?" Mindy jiggled on the edge of her seat. Her hand bumped the carton that covered the house, taking up a good half of the table.

"Careful," her father cautioned. "That thing may be worth a fortune. You see," he said almost reluc-

tantly, "either the little table isn't doll furn.
it's made from a kind of wood that doesn't exist.

Mindy and her mother looked at him blankly.

He grinned and ran his fingers through his hair. "My reaction exactly. I can't explain it, but this little table is made of . . . well, I guess you'd call it 'miniature wood.' But there *is* no such thing. Even bonsai, the Japanese miniature trees, grow wood cells of normal size. The grain in this table *looks* exactly like pine, but the cells are incredibly small." He drew a deep breath and said in a joking tone, "Now, unless the wood's from some exotic, unknown tree, this was once a full-size kitchen table."

"Oh, Jack, and here I thought you were serious!" Laughing, Mrs. Hallam began to remove the dessert things from the table. "I haven't had my leg so well pulled in ages!"

"You mean real furniture *shrunk?*" Mindy giggled. "You're two months late for April Fool, Daddy!"

"So I am, so I am." He laughed off his puzzlement with an effort. "Riddles aside, this Mr. Putt of yours who has an eye out for doll furniture seems to be hanging around here like a fly around a honey pot. I don't like it at all. Of course, he could have heard about the house from anyone who went to the Warnecki sale. But he must have an idea of its value to be making such a nuisance of himself."

"Why doesn't he just ask about it outright?" Mindy said. "Why should he be so sneaky?"

A hesitant knock rattled the screen door. "Yoohoo!"

All three Hallams jumped. All three darted looks

toward the carton-covered house. Any visitor would think it an awkwardly large and very unlikely table decoration.

"Oh, Mrs. Bright. It's you!"

"No, no. I mustn't come in," Mrs. Bright protested as Mr. Hallam rose. "I hear my teakettle whistling, and I must hurry back to it. I only thought you ought to know, Mr. Hallam."

Mr. Hallam's eyebrows shot up in a comical fashion. "Know that your teakettle is whistling?"

Mrs. Bright laughed, a silvery ripple of amusement. "Dear me, no." A worried frown came back to wrinkle her forehead and make her look more than ever like an elderly pixie. "It's that dreadful little man who tried to sell me a television aerial this afternoon. I told him I couldn't even afford a television *set*, but he *would* insist on climbing up on my roof. It put me in an awful tizzy. Now he's back, and poking along your back hedge. I expect he's watching us this very minute."

"That does it!" Mr. Hallam pushed his chair back from the table, furious. "Nell, telephone Officer Beagle. I'll get Horace out of his pen, and we'll settle this right now. Mindy, out of the way!"

"Oh dear, oh dear, oh dear!" Mrs. Bright's eyes sparkled as the Hallams scattered.

"Come on, let's watch." The sound of the big dog's deep bark (Mindy fondly called him Horse, as short for Horace) and crashing noises from the hedge were more than Mindy could resist. She pulled Mrs. Bright out and across the back garden, but when they were halfway, another sound caught the old lady's ear.

"Fudge! It's my teakettle. I *mustn't* let it burn up, child. I burnt one up last week." She hurried away at a bustling, birdlike run, calling back over her shoulder, "Do come when it's over and tell me what happens. There's fresh chocolate layer cake for visitors." With a little ducking motion she disappeared through a hole in the side hedge.

Mindy stood, undecided, tempted by the sound of her father's shouting, Horse's distant barking, and Officer Beagle's siren wailing down the highway. Brittlesdale's policeman so rarely had any call to use the siren that when the least occasion presented itself, he overdid it and enjoyed himself immensely. But the other wail, Mrs. Bright's teakettle, had reminded Mindy of the dollhouse. It needed watching, too. She hurried back to the porch to stand guard over it with a golf club, feeling both faintly silly and considerably nervous.

Mrs. Bright cut another slice of the rich, dark cake. It was Mindy's fourth, counting dessert at home. But Mrs. Bright's layer cakes were, Mindy felt sure, the best in the world. Where else did you find the layers of icing almost as thick as the layers of cake?

Mindy went on with her story as she cut into her cake. "So he must've circled around to the highway and his truck. Anyhow, he zoomed out of sight before the constable could get his car turned around. Horse almost had a fit, he was so excited. He barked himself hoarse. Oh!" She giggled. "Horse barked himself hoarse. Is that a pun?" She took a large bite of cake.

"A 'play on words' perhaps, dear." But Mrs. Bright was only half listening. "Such a very odd little man."

She tilted her head to one side, a quizzical, bird-like gesture. "Do you know, he reminded me of a dreadful little person I knew when I was a girl. Willie Kurtz. Wilhelm Kurtz. Dear me, I haven't thought of that name in years! He drove a team of grays and a splendid big wagon, and sold patent medicines and marvelous cures for cancer and consumption—that sort of thing. All perfectly worthless, of course." She chuckled. "The man wanted me to marry him. Can you imagine?" She laughed to herself, remembering.

"How old were you?" asked Mindy, fascinated.

Mrs. Bright took a sip of tea. "Oh, seventeen or eighteen, I suppose. But, Mindy my dear, your little man doesn't interest me as does this dollhouse you think he may be after." Setting her cup and saucer on the coffee table, she perched excitedly on the edge of her chair. "Would the house have anything to do with the little pieces I saw in your front window this morning? The little settle and washstand? I've been thinking about them all day."

"Yes, they're from the house. Did you like them? They're not for sale, you know," she added hastily.

"Oh, I wasn't thinking of buying, my dear. It's only that . . ." She paused, remembering. "It's only that when I was a girl, we had just such a settle in our house, and a walnut washstand, too. The resemblance is . . . well, ours were made by my great-grandfather Buckle, and it occurred to me that he may have made miniatures of them, too. He had six daughters, and when they married and left home, one could have taken the doll furniture and the dollhouse. If my great-grandfather did make them, that is. Do you have any idea where your house came from originally?"

"All we know is we found it at Warneckies', over beyond Mosstown, at a farm sale."

Mrs. Bright was disappointed. "No. None of our kin ever lived over Mosstown way. And I was so sure! The pattern on the cushion on the little settle? It was faded, but it looked for all the world like the one Mama embroidered for our settle. And the brass handles on the washstand . . ."

"Your great-grandfather must've been awfully good with his hands," Mindy ventured cautiously, remembering her father's doubts.

"Oh, yes. My grandpa—his only son—used to say he could do anything. Woodworking, blacksmithing . . . everything."

"And he had seven children?" Mindy looked around the tiny cottage. "I thought you had always lived right here."

"Here, but not *here*." Mrs. Bright laughed. "Dear me, no. This was only the coach house in those days. After I married Mr. Bright, we remodeled it, and since we never had children, I never truly missed the big house. This little nest was just perfect." She smiled mistily, remembering; then recollected herself and cut a tiny sliver more of cake.

"What I *did* miss was the books," she said. "Mama never could resist a book salesman, and so Papa had to build wide bookcases on each side of our front parlor door to hold all of the sets she bought—Dickens and Macaulay and George Eliot—ever so many. I always said I was going to read my way through them all, but I never made it past the second shelf." She sighed.

Mindy found swallowing suddenly very difficult. The cake stuck in her throat as she remembered afternoon sunlight in a cheerful parlor, sunlight falling on . . .

She coughed and managed to croak, "Did . . . did the bookcases have glass doors?"

"Why, yes. As I recall, they did, dear." the old lady eyed her curiously. "What *is* the matter, Mindy?"

Mindy took a deep breath to forestall the hiccup she felt coming. "Whatever happened to the house?"

"The house?" Mrs. Bright faltered. She looked dimly perplexed and sounded almost evasive. "Oh, the house was torn down years ago. It used to stand where your father's barn-studio is now."

Mindy persisted. "Was it a stone house? And did you have an Oriental carpet and a chandelier in your front parlor?"

"Yes. Yes, we did. But why, child?"

"Then your great-grandfather *did* make it!" Mindy jumped up from the sofa, cracking her shin on the coffee table in the rush of excitement. "He *did* make my house. It has to be his! Oh, do come see it, Mrs. Bright. Can you come now? Daddy put it in the workroom in the barn because the windows there are too high up for that Mr. Putt to peek in, unless he gets up on your roof again. *Please* come."

"Very well, Mindy dear." Mrs. Bright clapped her hands together. "I'll just fetch my sweater. Why, I declare, this is like Christmas!" She darted upstairs and in a moment was down again, swathed in a fluffy pink sweater decorated with orange flowers. "My after-dark sweater," she explained. "My niece in California sent it, and I *do* love it because it's warm as toast. But it is a wee bit conspicuous for daytime in Brittlesdale."

Mindy was already out the door and flying down the flagstone walk.

"I'll get the keys," she called.

The new padlock on the barn door was stubborn. As Mindy jiggled the key back and forth, Mrs. Bright gave a little gasp of amusement.

"Mindy dear, how silly of us! Great-Grandfather Buckle could hardly have made your house. He was dead ages before Papa built the bookcases or Mama embroidered that cushion. My, oh! I wonder if Cousin Delmer could have made it? He was always carving little things—little baskets out of peach pits and that sort of thing."

The padlock gave way at last.

"There!" Mindy let Mrs. Bright go in first, then relocked the door with the bolt on the inside.

The house sat under a card table in the middle of the room in a pool of light from the streetlamp outside the high windows.

"The card table was my idea," Mindy explained as she pulled it away. "So Mr. Putt couldn't see the house even if he got up to the windows with a ladder. It just fit. If I can find the pull string, we can have some more light."

She groped for the string, all the while watching Mrs. Bright expectantly.

"Oh, la!" said Mrs. Bright, very faintly indeed. "Dear *me!* It is our house. It is, it is, it *is!*"

She bent over, then got down on her knees in the pool of light to peer in the upstairs windows. It was too dark inside to see anything, but the fanlight over the front door, the knocker, and the doorknob itself drew her fluttering fingers.

"Look at this, Mindy," she whispered. "This is the B on the doorknob that Great-Grandfather Buckle made."

Mrs. Bright touched the doorknob with a hesitant finger. As she did so, Mindy felt a strange, painful ringing in her ears. She clapped her hands over them and squeezed her eyes tightly shut, but the ringing sound grew still louder. She did not actually see what happened, but it felt as if the barn had exploded outward. She found herself flat on her back under her father's heavy workbench in a rushing wind. There was the sound of falling debris on all sides. She huddled under the bench.

It was quiet again in a minute. When Mindy sat up and opened her eyes, there was Mrs. Bright, rigid with amazement, kneeling in the twilight on the front step of her old home, both hands gripping the doorknob marked B. Very slowly she pulled herself up and very slowly turned the knob. The door swung open.

"W-won't you come in, Mindy dear?" Her voice quavered.

Somewhere off to the side of the house a timber from the Hallam barn groaned and toppled with a crash.

Mindy's knees felt like water, but she stood and followed.

Four

"Well, I declare!" Mrs. Bright came to an abrupt stop at the end of the dark hall, one hand grasping Mindy's and the other holding open the door into the kitchen. "Whatever . . . ?"

The kitchen was not dark. The kitchen, in fact, was washed with the half-light of dusk and open to all outdoors. Three walls—the fireplace end, the side where the cupboards and hall door stood, and the end that opened into the pantry—were solid-looking, but the missing fourth wall gave everything a make-believe look.

"Whatever has happened to the back door?" Mrs. Bright frowned. "That will never do." She clucked.

Mindy blinked in amazement and admiration. A tiny house burgeoned into a full-size house in a matter of moments, and though Mrs. Bright was concerned, she didn't seem in the least bewildered.

Aplomb. That was what Mrs. Bright had: aplomb. She might be surprised, but she did not flap. It was very reassuring. Even so, for a moment the thought passed through Mindy's head that she was asleep and dreaming. "I'm dreaming. I went to bed, and all that cake is giving me dreams." But she did not convince herself. Everything was too solid. She moved farther into the kitchen, to stare out into the littered yard. The barn *had* been splintered flat. The slat-back chair she held onto was real to the touch—worn smooth with use, its seat covered with a cushion a foot square. The cushion was still damp from yesterday's cleaning. Yesterday, when it had been what? About an inch square?

Lights shone in the Hallam house, across the rose garden. Horace's deep bark sounded from his pen out back.

"I wonder why your father hasn't come out," Mrs. Bright said. "That was such a dreadful noise. Surely he must have heard it?"

"They're not there," Mindy explained. She was glad to have something ordinary to test her voice on. Even so, it squeaked a little. "They were going up to Georgiatti's for a while."

"Perhaps it's just as well," murmured the little old lady. "I shouldn't be able to explain. I shall need to think a bit. I mean, it *is* lovely to have the dear old house back, but it's dreadfully embarrassing about your father's poor barn."

"To have the house . . . *back?*" Mindy was not perfectly sure that Mrs. Bright knew what she was talking about. To be back, something had to have been away; and Mrs. Bright had not even known about the dollhouse before today. Let alone a dollhouse that grew like a mushroom when you touched the front doorknob. Perhaps she had been hit on the head by a falling roof tile or something.

"Yes, dear, 'back.'" The old lady had turned to rummage in a drawer of the cabinet beside the door. "You see, it disappeared in 1915 while we were in California. No one saw it go, and there was nothing left when we returned but the basement. It's obvious what's happened. It's simply come back the way it went. Some sort of slippage in time and space, perhaps. I'm sure we shall find that there is a perfectly rational explanation."

"You mean, it's truly your *real* house?" Mindy faltered. "A-and not a . . . magical dollhouse?"

"Tut! Magic, indeed! As if there weren't marvels enough without magic. Pictures traveling by telephone, and men bouncing up and down on the moon? Trees and flowers and children growing? There are your *real* marvels. This one has a perfectly simple explanation, I shouldn't wonder. Ah, here we are! Just where Mama always kept them." Mrs. Bright flourished a half-empty box of kitchen candles. "And there are still some lucifers in the jar."

Taking a match from a screw-top jar, Mrs. Bright struck it on a small square of sandpaper glued to a tin backing that said STRIKE HERE and was fastened on the inside of the cabinet door. The match flared. The candle caught, then guttered until the old lady found a candle holder and had a hand free with which to shield the flame.

"Come along, dear. I must see everything. Oh, it's been so very long! And isn't this exciting?" Mrs. Bright beckoned Mindy toward the hall door.

In the doorway she hesitated, turning to peer out again through the kitchen into the fast-darkening garden. "What I *cannot* understand is where that back wall can have gotten to. There were two windows and a door. *Most* peculiar."

Mindy gathered her wits. If Mrs. Bright thought such a—such a happening was all quite natural, perhaps there really was nothing to get in a flap about. She fought down the urge to make a run for the garden and tried very hard to sound matter of fact as she followed Mrs. Bright out into the hall.

"Daddy must've left the back off when he put the cleaned furniture in again," Mindy said. "I hope it didn't get smashed in the . . . explosion. I didn't see it out there."

Mrs. Bright stopped with one foot on the bottom stair. In the candlelight Mindy saw a faint frown wrinkle her forehead. "Left the back off? What *are* you chattering about, child? You can't mean that your father tore the back off my poor old house just to have a peek in? That doesn't sound a bit like careful John Hallam."

"Oh, no," Mindy protested. "You see, before it was, well . . . unshrunk, your house here *was* a dollhouse. At least, it had a back that came off. Didn't you see how the whole thing was fastened on a board? Well, in the rear there was a slot and a little catch-thing to hold the back on."

"How could that be?" Mrs. Bright backed up to the Windsor settee farther along the hall and sat down with a *plump* and an unhappy look. She set the candlestick down beside her. "Now I *am* muddled, Mindy dear. I could understand a simple shrink-and-unshrink. Or at least I could *conceive* of a shrink-and-unshrink. But it is our old house and *not* a dollhouse. It was strange enough to think the back wall *lost,* but however could it come to have a back that hooks on? It makes no sense at all. Why, everything else is just as I remember it. This is the settee where I used to drop my school books. And that is dear old Uncle Hezekiah." She patted the seat beside her and pointed with the other hand to a framed portrait drawn in charcoal hanging on the wall opposite. It was a stiff but kindly gentleman with mutton-chop whiskers and a faintly cross-eyed look.

Mindy was saved from a poorly smothered giggle by the sudden return of Mrs. Bright's good spirits. "Not to worry!" she chirped. The house itself was too much for her to resist. Snatching up the candle once more, she pattered up the stairs with Mindy close at her heels.

"Mind the top step, dear. There's a snag where Papa caught his foot in the runner the night the bat got in and Papa went after it with a shotgun. Poor Papa! He was so *dread*fully angry and looked so silly in his nightcap, blazing away indoors. The bat got away, and . . . look! Yes, there it is." She held the

light up and pointed high up on the rose-papered wall. A large patch of the wallpaper was pitted and torn as if by a discharge of buckshot at close range.

A little sigh escaped Mrs. Bright. "Dear Papa! That was the week before we left for San Francisco and the Exposition. We called them expositions in those days, not world's fairs," she explained as she bustled along the upper hall toward the front of the house. "My, oh! The Lincoln Highway was just new, and we simply sailed along. We had a Kissel Kar. Fancy my remembering that! I wonder why they ever stopped making Kissel Kars. Very comfortable, it was. It was a lovely Exposition. And did you know that the tracks for the San Francisco cable cars were made right here? Right up in Johnstown, that is?" Pushing open the door on her right, she beckoned Mindy in.

It was a bedroom—a girl's bedroom. Mrs. Bright's own, Mindy guessed as she saw the dressing glass stuck around with faded photographs and programs, and bits of ribbon, and dried flowers pinned onto rosettes of paper lace. At Mrs. Bright's cottage next door, all of the mirrors were decorated with snapshots and clippings and greeting cards. Here, the bed was a large four-poster with a canopy of embroidered linen.

"Golly, how neat! Has it got the kind of curtains you can pull shut?" Mindy forgot everything in her excitement over the bed. She had always dreamed of having a tester bed or a cupboard bed. You could shut yourself up in your own cozy little world and let everything outside go on just as it wished without you. The curtains pulled smoothly along their rods on little wooden rings. "How *neat!*" she repeated.

Mrs. Bright perched on the needlepoint-covered stool in front of her old vanity table and sniffed sentimentally as she went through the faded and yellowed souvenirs so long ago tucked around the rim of her dressing glass. Of a mashed and sadly crumbling wad of crepe paper, she murmured, "My goodness! One of the nut cups Alma Stahl made for the Christian Endeavor picnic supper at Findlay Park Lake! Alma's nut cups never change, sad to say. At the last Ladies' Circle meeting, we had little May baskets just like this. Oh . . . !" She gasped. "Oh, *dear* William. Sweet William." She felt in her pocket for a handkerchief and dabbed at two tears rolling down her pink and wrinkled cheeks.

It was a small card, picture-postcard size, hand-painted in watercolors but so warped and blurred that Mindy could not make out what the original picture might have been. Little Mrs. Bright dimpled and brushed a small hand through her white curls.

"Mr. Bright painted it. The sweetest birthday card I ever had. See here, what it says across the bottom? 'To the sweetest flower of May.' My name is Mary, but Mr. Bright always called me May. And this blur that looks like a wobbly green umbrella? That is . . . *was* a mayflower leaf. But down here where the flower and the little mayapple bloom? He painted . . . dear me, let me think . . . yes, forget-me-nots and orange blossoms instead. I had so many beaux that dear William was very nervous about asking me to marry him. He sent me this as a sort of hint, you see."

Mindy made a polite noise that meant, "I bet it was pretty," and handed it back. "How did it get all blurry like that?" she asked.

"It fell in the lake . . ." Mrs. Bright began.

"Oh, ork! Is *this* yours?" Mindy broke into the old lady's remembering, her hand darting out to a rounded glass object on the vanity table. "Where's it from?"

It was a pretty little paperweight of a lovely opaque blue glass with "windows," round openings in the blue through which you looked into the clear glass to a colorful mushroom-shaped mound of brightly colored glass flowers. Millefiori. Mindy's mother had explained that millefiori taken literally meant "a thousand flowers," but really meant just such a cluster as this. The thin outer layer of blue glass must be the blue named after the king of Clichy, and the clump of blossoms could certainly be called a "mushroom millefiori center." Mindy blinked and wrenched her gaze away. It was almost as if she were about to fall, to float down through one of the windows in the blue, float down through the clear, no-longer solid glass to rest on that mound of scarlet and blue and yellow—not closely packed circlets of colored glass, but morning glories and glowing poppies.

"That? *That* is why dear Mr. Bright's little picture fell into Findlay Park Lake." Mrs. Bright smoothed a bent corner of the old card as she told about the day of the picnic. That morning, it seemed, the dreadful Willie Kurtz had come to call, and she, Miss Mary Buckle, had been trapped. Usually her mama, or one of the cousins, gave warning when his shiny Hupmobile chugged into sight so that Miss Mary had time to snatch up a novel to read before she slipped out into the orchard and up an apple tree. This time she was fairly caught. There was nothing to do but ask Willie Kurtz into the front parlor. It was awful. Refusing an offer of milk and cookies, he had straightaway insisted that Miss Mary elope with him across the state line to Cumberland that very afternoon. "My little bus can make the trip in two hours, sweetie," he had said, smiling with all his teeth. "We'll have the knot tied and be back in time for supper with your folks." When an alarmed Miss Buckle had objected that she had to go to the church picnic that afternoon, Wilhelm Kurtz had sneered. "Who cares about a passel of psalm-singing ninnies frisking around with shuttlecocks and canoes?" Miss Buckle had faltered and grasped at a straw. "But I am supposed to bring the baked beans and a Sunshine cake," she said, and for some reason that had encouraged Mr. Kurtz.

"I suppose," Mrs. Bright said thoughtfully, "it must have sounded a very halfhearted excuse. At any rate, he produced this little paperweight, very prettily done up in tissue paper and lace ribbon. Do you know, it was so exquisite that I was very naughty and kept it. It was very foolish of me, for poor old Willie Kurtz thought it meant that I had accepted *him*. I traipsed off to the picnic full of tender feelings for William Bright, with his dear birthday card tucked inside my bodice, but this pretty little glass frippery was weighting down my skirt pocket. I was very young and silly." Mrs. Bright laughed. "Dear William proposed in a canoe on Findlay Lake, and I was utterly, perfectly happy, weeping away like a waterworks. Then, for lack of a hankie I dried my tears on my skirt, and the paperweight rolled out and into the water. I quite lost my head and nearly tipped the canoe over. Fortunately the water was shallow, or more would have been drenched than William's pretty sketch. He had to rescue it, and the glass ball, and very nearly me. You may imagine how furious Willie Kurtz was when he heard that I had accepted William Bright. My, but he sputtered! Papa used to imitate him yelling, 'And here I was going to name my new machine after you: the Mary Kurtz Wart and Malignant Growth Reducer! The very best of all my medical machines! This one truly *works!* You shall regret this day, Miss Mary Buckle!'"

"*Wart* Reducer?" Mindy collapsed across the bed in a fit of giggles. "He must've been awfully gicky," she wheezed.

"I'm not sure what 'gicky' is, but he *was* strange, even . . . yes, frightening. It may *sound* silly now. It was alarming at the time."

Mindy frowned. "You know how you said all his teeth showed when he smiled? Mr. Putt's do, too. Do you suppose *he* could be your Mr. Kurtz?" She explained about Mr. Putt and the paperweight.

"How odd. But no, he's far too young," Mrs.

Bright objected. "Willie Kurtz would be nearly eighty, and your Mr. Putt didn't look a day over fifty." She fell silent, then after a moment said thoughtfully, "Still, the house did disappear that very summer, while we were away. It was such a shock to everyone in Brittlesdale, *such* a mystery, that everyone avoided mentioning it at all. Now-you-see-it-now-you-don't is very alarming on a large scale. The most polite thing hereabouts was to pretend it hadn't happened."

The little old lady's musings were broken off by a rapid succession of loud noises that seemed to explode just outside the bedroom window: the roar of a badly muffled exhaust, crashing footsteps, and Horace's loud belling bark. The bark sounded closer and closer, strangely deep.

"Now how did he get out of his pen?" Mindy began. "He shouldn't be . . ."

At that moment the house gave a violent lurch. There was a deafening clap of wood against wood, and the bedroom door flew open in a rush of air.

The candle blew out.

Most alarming of all was the sensation that followed. Mindy had felt it before. But that had been while going up in a very fast elevator in a tall Pittsburgh hotel.

Five

"It's an earthquake!" Mrs. Bright panted, wild-eyed, as the house rocked. Upstairs and down, the glass and crockery that was not already on the floor tumbled from tables and cupboards. The big tester bed rolled around the bedroom on its casters. "In the doorway! Safest place!" Mrs. Bright called as the house tilted again. She half ran and half skated to the door and clung there.

The bark sounded deafeningly close, and the house bucked like a bronco. Mindy dodged the bed and lunged her way to the front window, where she caught hold of the handle at the bottom of the sash. Lifting her head above the sill, she peered out.

"Oh, Mrs. Bright! It's not an earthquake. It's Mr. Putt! Oomph! Hold on!"

Mindy could not manage another word. Holding on took all of her strength. Outside the window a giant world was lurching and swaying, and a gigantic Horace barked frantically, lunging at the incredible coat sleeve that brushed across the window frame.

In a moment the light was gone and the monstrous nightmare landscape with it. A loud scraping sound, a lurch to one side, and the starting up of a powerful car engine followed one another in quick succession. The house settled down to a rhythmic jiggle. Mindy picked herself up from the floor, but a speechless Mrs. Bright still clutched at the doorjamb.

"I think," said Mindy very slowly, blinking owlishly, "I think we're in the back of Mr. Putt's truck. I think . . . I think *we've* just been shrunk by some kind of Super Wart Reducer."

"Oh, surely not." Mrs. Bright groped her way across the dark room to Mindy's side. Together, they managed to raise the sash. The air outside was stuffy, and they caught a faint whiff of exhaust fumes. The steady throb of the motor was the only sound beside the occasional rushing roar of a passing car.

Mrs. Bright made a small clucking sound. "I do believe you are right, child. We are in a truck. There's no mistaking the smell. We are in a truck. How very odd! We are being housenapped."

"What'll we do?" Mindy whispered. Her head whirled.

"First of all," said Mrs. Bright practically, "we will put the window down again. I can't abide gasoline fumes. They give one a headache. Then . . .

since we cannot very well escape from a closed van whizzing along at what must be seventy miles an hour, I suggest that we go to bed. We shall need our rest if we are to do anything sensible in the morning."

So, feeling rather silly, they went to bed. First, however, they lifted the legs of the old four-poster one by one and removed the casters. Then Mrs. Bright stripped off the dusty coverlet and brought clean—if not fresh—sheets and blankets from a blanket chest in the hall.

They could not risk showing a light, and so Mrs. Bright had to work by "feel" in the inky blackness, but her memory served her well. After trying several drawers in a tall chest-on-chest, she brought out two long nightgowns, ruffled at the neck and wrists.

"There! We might as well be comfortable. Never mind if it's a little large, dear. Just roll up the cuffs." Mrs. Bright pulled the bed-curtains shut all around.

Once snuggled down beside Mrs. Bright, Mindy began to laugh. It began deep down, and before long the bed was shaking with their laughter.

"Oh my, but it isn't really funny at all," Mrs. Bright gasped. "It's perfectly absurd!"

"I guess I shouldn't laugh," said Mindy, sobering. "If Mama and Daddy are home from Georgiatti's, they must be frantic. I mean, what would *you* think if you came home to all that and found us gone?"

"They will be very frightened. But it does no good to fret about what you cannot mend," Mrs. Bright said firmly. "Tomorrow we shall find our bearings and try to think of a way to get word to them."

"Daddy will guess it's Mr. Putt's doing," Mindy said, feeling somewhat reassured. "Do you know, he *said* this was a real house, and Mama and I just laughed."

"Your father is a man of sense. Now, we must be sensible, too. Go to sleep, and in the morning we shall have ourselves a think. We should be safe for a while, at least, for I doubt your Mr. Putt guesses he has added peoplenapping to his housenapping. Good night, my dear."

And so they went to sleep in a jiggling old tester bed, in a house two-and-a-half feet high, shut up in the back of a television repair van speeding eastward through the moonlit hills.

Mindy sat up with a start. The bed-curtains were open on Mrs. Bright's side, and the faint light of early morning washed across the faded fields of daisies on the wallpaper. Mrs. Bright was already up and about. The long white nightgown lay neatly folded on her pillow.

Mindy rubbed her eyes, flopped back, and stretched as hard as she could. The dream just before waking had been of awakening to a breakfast of her mother's buttermilk pancakes drenched in maple syrup. No such luck. Vaguely she remembered how they had stopped wherever here was, in the middle of the night. There had been the clanging of the doors on the back of the truck, the awful bucketing swaying again, and then bright light—

electric light—pouring through the windows. Mindy and Mrs. Bright had clung to the bedposts and felt very thankful for the heavy bed-curtains that hid them.

Mindy clambered across the bed and out. Even now it would be wiser to stay away from the windows, she knew, but curiosity got the better of her. Edging up to the side window, she took a quick look. The view did not tell much. The huge room outside was still shadowy in the early dawn. Through a wide picture window in the wall opposite, Mindy saw sky and trees tipped with the sunrise, and, still in shadow, the familiar panel truck. Such a giant world! And *why* did the mysterious Mr. Putt want a house badly enough to steal it? Her heart thumped with alarm as a chipmunk appeared on the sill of the wide picture window. It was as tall as she was. And on chipmunk level, the thing that impressed you most was not how cute they were, but what big teeth they had. Mindy shivered and hurried to get dressed. Mrs. Bright would be downstairs. She *hoped* Mrs. Bright was downstairs. What if Mr. Putt had a cat, and . . .

"Now, Araminta, be sensible," she said to herself, in imitation of Mrs. Bright. "Don't waste your worrying on maybes."

Something—perhaps the remembered aroma of dream pancakes and syrup at the back of her mind —sent her to look in the kitchen first. But she pulled the kitchen door shut as quickly as she had opened it. The back of the house was still off, or had been removed again upon their arriving. But then, even if the kitchen had been safe, it had no breakfast to offer. Mindy sighed and tried not to think of food.

Mrs. Bright was in the dining room, at the front of the house across the hall from the parlor. The heavy, lined brocade drapes that had prevented the Hallams from seeing in were now a welcome protection from prying eyes. Mrs. Bright had pinned them securely together so that no crack of light would show and sat at the table calmly reading *Felix Holt* by candlelight.

"Good morning, Mindy dear." She twinkled as cheerfully as ever as she put the book down and motioned Mindy to the chair opposite. "I've waited breakfast for you, you see."

Two places had been set, and in the middle of each plate was a cellophane-wrapped butterscotch toffee.

"I found four pieces in my sweater pocket," she explained. "The other two will do for lunch if we can't arrange for something better by then. I *am* sorry it is so little. I was *very* reckless and searched the kitchen and pantry. There are a few tins of things like deviled ham and pork and beans and evaporated milk, but I didn't like to clatter through the silverware drawer looking for the can opener. If they aren't all spoiled after fifty-odd years, as I suppose they must be, we will be very lucky. Mama's lovely jars of fruits and preserves are ruined, of course—shriveled up hard as rocks even with paraffin over them and the lids sealed."

"Well, I hope we won't *be* here past lunch."

Mrs. Bright looked slightly less cheerful. "Tell me, dear, have you taken a peek outside?"

"Um. From upstairs." Mindy spoke around the candy.

Mrs. Bright raised her eyebrows. "And you weren't surprised? You must have looked out the side window. *The* view is out the front. My oh, I hope you can make something of it, for I can't. No, no. Not there. I have the drapes pinned just right. Take a peek out of the front door. Then we will have to think what to do."

Much mystified, Mindy obeyed. At first she opened the front door only a crack, but then in her astonishment she drew it all the way open and stood and stared. Directly opposite, as far away, it seemed, as if it were across a small park or a wide highway, was a church. A church, at the end of a row of houses. And there was a house next door to the Buckle house—the same size. Far off to the right she saw the same huge window and door she had sighted through the upstairs window. A town? And indoors?

She stepped out into the dim morning, down the front steps, and onto a sandpapery sidewalk. The house next door was a handsome brick edifice, and the one beyond that was a small but elegant log house, beautifully built and carefully chinked. At the far end of the street more buildings were still in shadow.

The worst thing was, it was all faintly familiar. And *that* was stranger than the fact of there being a town indoors at all.

"I've been here before. Oh, I *know* it. I've been here *before*," she whispered fiercely to herself. The feeling of being on the edge of a dream grew. "Where? Where *is* it? *Did* I dream it?"

The answer came in a wash of light, and the nightmarish feeling faded. Outside the wide picture window the bright blue truck was touched by the sun. But the white sign was gone from its side. Bold black letters no longer announced L. L. PUTT, TELEVISION REPAIR. Instead, in buttercup yellow on the blue background, it read LILLIPUT U.S.A.; and underneath in smaller letters, THE MARVELOUS MUSEUM OF MINIATURES.

Mrs. Bright winced as Mindy slammed the front door and flung into the dining room.

"Oh, I forgot," she panted. "I'm sorry. But, oh, Mrs. Bright! *I know where we are.* I've been here before. It's at Lake Meander! You know, up northeast? We were here once when I was real little, on vacation. There are a lot of galleries and museums and shops and stuff, and this is one of them. Lilliput U.S.A. It's not a real town out there. It's all set up on a big old table, U-shaped, so you can see all the house fronts as if they were on three sides of a town square? And you can go around the backs and see inside 'cause they're all open there. I always thought it was a kind of neat place," she said lamely, running out of steam.

"I know exactly how you feel," said Mrs. Bright solemnly. "Lake Meander, is it? *I* have always wanted to visit Lake Meander."

"Well, we're here," Mindy said glumly. She sat down. "Do you suppose *all* these dollhouses are really housenapped houses? And did you see the truck? What do you bet it's like I guessed: his name's not L. L. Putt at all? He must've made that up out of Lilliput."

"I expect you're right, dear. But we aren't any nearer an explanation of why my house was stolen now or in the first place. We really must decide what's best to do. I'm sure Willie—if he is Wilhelm Kurtz, that is—I'm sure he has no idea he brought us away too. Perhaps when he awakens, we should simply announce ourselves and ask to be unshrunk?"

Mindy was doubtful. "Would he do it?"

"Oh, surely!" The little old lady hesitated. "But not . . . not if he knew I were Mary Buckle Bright. I sadly fear that Willie Kurtz would think it very funny to keep us here. He had a quite nasty streak to him. Unless of course," she went on doubtfully, "this could be Willie's son and not Willie? The resemblance is uncanny, but . . ."

Mindy was not listening. A strange detail, a faint sensation she had ignored in her excitement, had drifted back to her. In a tone of surprise she said suddenly, "I smelled toast—toast and coffee. Why should I smell toast and coffee out there? Unless . . . golly, Mrs. Bright, Whoever-he-is must be up already. Oh, what if he saw me?"

Mrs. Bright hurried to the rear wall and slid back a wooden panel. It was a pass-through for food and plates, and gave a view out through the kitchen. Stooping beside Mrs. Bright, Mindy saw a half-open door at the far side of the big museum room and a small untidy room beyond. Looking out into that oversize world through the narrow pass-through reminded Mindy of sitting up close to a wide-screen movie. She saw a hot plate on a littered table and the end of a huge brass bedstead where someone with very large feet was sleeping. His snoring was like the rumble of distant thunder.

"Then what did I smell?" Mindy hissed as Mrs. Bright slid the panel shut.

"Dear, I *do* hope it isn't something burning. Defective wiring, or something like that. How would we ever get down from this table you say we're on?"

Mindy led the way to the front door, and together they walked down to the painted and sanded sidewalk. It had grown light enough to see up to the end of the town, where there seemed to be shops and a bank.

"*Doesn't* it smell like toast?"

"Yes, dear. Toast, and freshly ground coffee. But it isn't of course. Perhaps we had better have a look around now, though, while our housenapper is asleep."

They walked along the painted green lawns, because the sidewalk was too crunchily noisy. The coarse grains of sand that had been glued to the tabletop to give the effect of a sanded walk seemed to them as large as heavy gravel. There were four houses between their own and the corner of the "street," and by the time they reached the last, the aroma of coffee was unmistakable.

"How very odd," whispered Mrs. Bright, holding tightly to Mindy's hand.

On the cross street there were the blank faces of a town hall, a bank, a fire house, and a general store. To Mindy's sharp eyes it looked as if the sign that said FIRST BANK OF LILLIPUT had once said FIRST BANK OF something else. Around the next corner was a large and rambling LILLIPUT INN, and after it along the third side of the great U-shaped table were several more houses and the church Mindy had seen at first.

"Oh!"

They both saw it at once.

From the center chimney of the inn ran a thin waver of heat: not smoke, but the rising shimmer from a fire made with the driest and hardest of wood and carefully watched.

Someone was cooking breakfast in the inn.

Six

The doorbell worked. It rang dimly somewhere inside the inn. Mindy and Mrs. Bright waited nervously on the doorstep for a moment before pulling at the bell handle again. The sound was scarcely a ghost of a ring, and neither Mindy nor the little old lady knew whether they hoped someone would answer or not—for if any . . . any*one* did, who or what could it be? They half feared (though neither admitted it) that the door would be flung open by a belligerent mouse. In the suspense of the moment they had forgotten the aroma of toast and coffee, or they would have been reassured. Even the most talented of the storybook mice of their acquaintance was not inclined to the toasting of bread and brewing of coffee.

A curtain fluttered at an upper window. Mindy caught the movement from the corner of her eye and nudged Mrs. Bright violently. They had a glimpse of a pale shadow that disappeared as the curtain was let fall.

"Whoever it is must be a sensible body," said Mrs. Bright, falling back on her favorite word. "And cautious. I expect he—or she—did not fancy opening the door to, say, a mouse. No more would I." She smoothed the front of her dress and tried to look calm and unruffled.

Soon footsteps could be heard approaching the door, and the sound of heavy bolts being drawn back, and door chains unhooked. After what seemed ages, the door creaked open, and a small, pale person ducked down in a rusty curtsy.

"Morning, ma'am, miss," the pale person whispered. Managing to raise her voice to a nervous croak, she added, "Welcome to Dopple Inn, and I'm to say, 'Won't you come in quick, please?'"

Mindy and Mrs. Bright obeyed, taking a last, still incredulous look back across the housetops opposite to the top of the half-open door of their unsuspecting captor's bedroom.

"This way, please," croaked the pale person once she had fastened up the door again. She started off at a scurry toward the wide stairway at the back of the shadowy entrance hall.

"Wait a minute!" Mindy called. "Hey, who are you? Does anybody else live here?"

"This way please." The pale person bobbed another curtsy and was off up the stairs at full speed. She was quite old, they had seen, white-haired and stooped over with arthritis or rheumatism. Her pale eyes had squinted and watered in the dim morning light that fell in at the front door. Here, trotting up the dark stair and down dark hallways, she was too fast for Mindy and Mrs. Bright, who would have been glad of a lamp or candle. Realizing at last that she had left them behind in the maze of the rambling old inn, the pale old creature came trotting back for them.

"This way, please." She repeated the words testily into the darkness, adding with a grudging politeness, "I'm Sybilla."

"And very like one, too," Mrs. Bright muttered, catching her breath. She did not explain what she meant, and Mindy made a mental note to look up what a sybilla might be the next time she saw a dictionary.

Sybilla led them down another, narrower set of stairs, around several corners (or, as Mrs. Bright had half suspected upstairs, around the same corners several times), and stopped at last by a door barely visible in the gloom. The lettering on the door dimly spelled out LAUNDRY.

"Well, here y'are," Sybilla said. Opening the door, she announced, "It's that house come back, and these've come with it, I warrant. Oh, it's OK. I checked from up top before I answered the door. The Prof ain't awake yet."

The announcement was made to the seven startled people who sat at breakfast around a table once meant for ironing and folding linens. It was an elderly gentleman in a faded fuzzy brown suit that looked as if it had been made from a blanket, who acknowledged the introduction.

"Th-thank you, Sybilla. And welcome, dear ladies, to our fair town of Dopple." He spoke formally, and his voice quavered from age and excitement. "I am Augustus Dopple."

The windowless laundry room and the eight inhabitants of Dopple looked exceedingly strange. The room had the look of an overcrowded burrow —shelves crammed with books, tools, cooking utensils, beloved knickknacks, and the inn's towels and sheets and tablecloths—and the inhabitants had the pale and pinched look of burrow dwellers too long shut away from the sun. As introductions were made all around, they stared, fascinated, at Mrs. Bright's red cheeks and weather-browned skin. Mindy they almost shied away from, as if they feared she might bite.

The very erect and disapproving old lady to Mr. Augustus Dopple's right was a Miss Britomart Umstott. She inclined her head only slightly as Mr. Dopple introduced her. "Spoiled," was Mrs. Bright's private opinion. Miss Umstott's pink muslin dress (very artfully made from a sheet and dyed with berry juice as they later learned) was primly high-necked and reached to her ankles. The face beneath the elaborately twisted coronet of white hair was still pretty—even girlish—but it wore a fretful look every bit as uncomfortable as Sybilla's sour one. Next to her was Mr. Herman Goff, a stout gentleman in an untidy pale blue suit that looked like a cross between pajamas, blanket, and tent. The clownlike effect of his shape and his suit was emphasized by a combination of pasty white skin and a red nose and even redder cheeks. Such a nose and cheeks might have been cheerful on a man of ruddy complexion. On Mr. Goff they looked feverish. He, after a shy "How-de-do," returned to a feverish consumption of toast. Next came Mr. Jack Crump, splendid

in a bristling moustache and a bush of faded red hair. Once the cook and now manager of the Dopple Inn, Mr. Crump rose, bowed, swallowed, and "allowed as he was charmed." Sybilla, it seemed, was Mrs. Crump.

After Mr. Crump came the Reverend Artemus Edwards, dignified even in a suit of ill-fitting gray blanket stuff and a very squashy clerical collar. Mindy found herself thinking that he must be the

kind of preacher who had a handshake like a glove full of moist mush. Finding his pale blue eyes frowning fierce disapproval at her, she blushed.

"Aw, it's OK, dearie. The Revver don't mean to eat you. He's only nearsighted." Fat Mrs. Eada Morrissey nudged her neighbor mockingly and squinted until her eyes disappeared in her puffy face. "The better to see you with, my dear!" She chortled and shook under her billowing white dressing gown like a very large and wobbly blancmange.

The Reverend winced and cast his eyes piously heavenward.

"*Dopple?* Dopple!" exclaimed Mrs. Bright, as if she could not take so much in one swallow. Vaguely she recalled or imagined she recalled hearing—ever so long ago—of a town of some such name. Hadn't the earth opened up and swallowed a town named Dopple? Or was she thinking of one of the little mining towns up near Scranton that had fallen down a caved-in mine shaft? No matter. By this time both Mrs. Bright and Mindy were very alarmed and distressed. There had to be a way out of their predicament! How long had these people *been* here? They were frightening in their timidity. A week, a day even, in the company of these dreadful, pale, whispery, ghostly people would be too shrinking to the spirit for comfort.

Just as they were close to tears, Mr. Dopple said, "And this is the last and least of us, little Samantha Bostweiler."

"Little" Samantha scraped her chair forward from behind Mrs. Morrissey's, and all glumness was gone.

"*Gosh,* am I glad to see you! Who *are* you?

Where'd you come from? And what a . . . a *lovely* sweater, Mrs. Bright! It was 'Mrs. Bright,' didn't you say? Oh, I've a million questions! But first off, how did the Prof ever come to snatch you?"

"Dear Samantha, such slang!" lamented the upright Miss Umstott. Apologetically she explained that "Samantha, I fear, spends too many of her evenings across the way watching Professor Kurtz's . . . *television.*" Miss Umstott managed to make the word sound distasteful.

"Heck, how else are we going to find out what goes on outside?" Samantha turned, chattering on as if someone had opened a faucet. *"Forty-five* years! Can you imagine? Fifty-five years in all, and forty-five of 'em here, and it's only the last ten that old fraud's had a TV. Forty-odd years with no more news than we got from the headlines of the Prof's newspapers. And those we had to read off the floor half the time, through my daddy's field glasses. Oh, I've just been waiting . . ."

"Dear Samantha, you must not agitate so," chided the Reverend Edwards. He clucked infuriatingly. "Our Samantha forgets from time to time that children should be seen and not heard."

Mindy stared. Mrs. Bright gave an incredulous snort. Samantha had to be in her late fifties, and might have been sixty or more. Samantha was tall and stringy, and if she was not as brown as Mrs. Bright, who spent much of her day in gardening, her skin had a warm golden look that did not come from hiding indoors. Her salt-and-pepper gray hair was cut short, and her practical dress—a red-and-white check that surely had once been a tablecloth

—came to just above the knee. Where the older residents of Lilliput U.S.A. or Dopple or whatever-it-was wore floppy slippers made from Turkish toweling, Samantha was barefoot.

Mrs. Bright recovered herself and shot a meaningful glance at Mindy. "Mindy, dear? Perhaps you and . . . Miss Samantha could fetch those tins of food from the Buckle house? Before Willie Kurtz wakes and takes it into his head to redd up that kitchen?" Her look said just as plainly as words, "And find out everything you *can*. Miss Samantha looks the most sensible of the lot."

"Oh, if it makes them feel better to keep thinking of me as a child, I don't mind," Samantha said cheerfully as she poked through the Buckle cupboards. "This is no kind of life for anybody, and after the first couple of years when they were still trying to figure a way out, why, it got to be every day was like every other day. I think they only lasted this long, poor dears, because, you see, if nothing ever changes, it's easier to pretend time's not passing and you're really not older. Except for the aches and pains. Dear old Nurse Morrissey is *so* crippled up. . . . Me, I'm lucky. And I was only five when the Prof stole Dopple—five and ornery. *Still* ornery. But definitely not five." She grinned.

While they gathered the cans and salt and candles, Samantha pieced the story together for Mindy from the bits and pieces she had heard in her childhood.

Seven

Late in the summer of 1915 a little man named Wilhelm Kurtz drove into the prosperous little town of Dopple in his shiny Hupmobile. He had set himself up in a small office above the general store, explaining, "Tired of being on the road, tired of doctoring everything from burns to bunions. This is a nice little burg," he said, "and I aim to put some roots down here." It was understood that Kurtz was a man of property, with a farm over beyond Mosstown. However, to the disappointment of middle-aged ladies with rheumatic twinges, he did no doctoring. The shiny brass nameplate on his door read PROFESSOR KURTZ, not "Doctor." Day in and day out he tinkered on a machine in the room above the store. "It takes up half that cubbyhole of his," said the electrician who had come in from Bedford to wire some of the more prosperous homes and businesses of Dopple. "Why, it's got little dials a-twitch all over. And do you know, he's got a little *doll's house* up there? He thought I wasn't lookin', but I saw the little pipsqueak tappin' all his fingers together and *laughin'* at it. Gloatin', you might say. If you was to ask me, I'd say he was minus a few marbles."

The more the Professor worked on the machine, the more desperate he must have become. Money was running short, for at last economy had prompted him to give up the little "office." Every penny must have gone to perfect the Kurtz Wart and Malignant Growth Reducer—except that, knowing by then it could shrink a house but not a wart, he began to call it simply the Reducer. He must have thought that if only he could understand the principle upon which it worked, he could devise precise controls. He brought his big old traveling-doctor wagon back from the farm where he had left it, half dismantled the machine so that he could get it out the door, and trundled it back to his farm. But every Saturday he reappeared, for he had begun to pay court to pretty Miss Britomart Umstott, daughter of the richest man in Dopple. When Miss Britomart gave him no encouragement, Kurtz had turned to Banker Dopple (father of the present Mr. Dopple). The banker was the second richest man in Dopple. "But all I need is five hundred dollars," pleaded the Professor. "And sure as eggs make little chickens, that little machine of mine will make me rich and you richer. It can't fail!" Yet, when pressed for details, he was always vague.

"Hum, well, um," he would say. "Uh, I intended it for a minor sort of medical treatment, but a-um, lighthearted experiment opened unexpected vistas. It works on a far larger scale than I had planned, but it is capricious, unpredictable. The difficulty is in the controls. Unreliable. But, once perfected, it will revolutionize . . . things. Say, the Transportation of Goods!"

Banker Dopple, a self-made man, was not about to buy a pig in a poke. Kurtz was not about to reveal his secret. No five hundred dollars. Kurtz had grown purple in the face and screamed, "A shortsighted, clutch-fisted old idiot, that's what you are! I'll show *you!*" and the banker had turned red as a beet and roared, "Out! Out! Out of my bank!"

That did it.

The next Saturday was the first day of the County Fair. Dopple looked deserted as it slumbered in the hot, dusty sunshine. No one stirred. Even the dogs had gone to the fair, hanging over wagon tailgates or riding joyfully in cars open to the breeze, grinning blissfully with eyes closed and ears streaming in the wind. The town looked deserted. But it wasn't. Not quite. Five-year-old Samantha Bostweiler was in bed with the chicken pox, eating forbidden chocolates from a box beneath her pillow, while Nurse Eada Morrissey dozed in a Boston rocker by the window. The rest of the Bostweilers had left for the fair in the cool of early morning. So, except for a few unfortunates, had the whole of the town of Dopple. And no one of the left-behinds actually *saw* what happened. Young Augustus Dopple, the banker's son, in the zeal of his First Week on the Job, was going over his bookkeeping accounts in the bank's inner office for the third time—Just to Be Sure. Pretty Miss Umstott was reclining on her pretty chaise longue in her pretty bedroom, nursing the nervous headache that had come on the day before when the odious Professor Kurtz had repeated—*and* repeated—his proposal of marriage. She had refused even more vigorously than before.

There were others, too. The Reverend Artemus Edwards did not approve of such frivolities as fairs and had been working all the morning on the words for a new hymn. It was to be called "The Voice Unheard," and the Reverend was so absorbed in it that for years afterward Herman Goff had called it "Wilhelm's Wagon Wheels Unheard." Mr. Goff, for his part, had heard the wagon rumble to a stop in front of the church, next door to the boarding house where he lived, but when you have two broken legs in casts, you think a while before letting curiosity get the better of you. Mr. Goff had fallen from the church steeple a few days before, having gone up to attach a new lightning rod.

Jack Crump and young Sybilla Butterbaugh had been hard at work in the kitchen of the Dopple Inn.

"Sybilla *Butterbaugh?*" Mindy interrupted. Samantha hugged the box of candles to her tablecloth dress. "Yes, the Reverend finally agreed to marry them after we settled down here in Lake Meander."

The inn, as with every County Fair opening day, expected a large turnout of weary fairgoers too tired to face cooking Saturday supper at home. Someone had to cook and someone had to scrape carrots and scour pots, so Mr. Crump and the shy Sybilla had been stuck. They were up to their elbows in the preparation of soup when the Profesor's wagon, a church and four houses already aboard, had drawn up in front of the Dopple Inn. There was no one to see the tailgate let down, the aiming of the fantastic machine, the methodical theft of another bit of Dopple. If Dopple would not support his research in one way, Kurtz would see that it did so in another. He had conceived of the idea of a traveling exhibit. There was money to be had in marvels. Just how much a marvel Dopple was, he would have been surprised to learn. He never did. All through the refurbishing of the houses to look like dollhouses, and the seven long years of traveling from one small town to another, and the years in busy Lake Meander, he never suspected that this housenapping had made him a peoplenapper, too.

"And of course when his dreadful nephew came to stay, we were twice as careful."

"Oh!" exclaimed Mindy, the light dawning. "This one is his nephew, then? Mrs. Bright didn't understand how her old Willie kept so young, but she didn't think it likely he would have had a son, either. Who would have *married* him? Gosh! They never *once* saw one of you? All those years?" Mindy dropped a pronged can opener into the laundry sack they were filling with things possibly edible and probably useful.

"No." Grimly Samantha added, "Young Willie had a kitten when we first came here. We saw how he tormented it. No, we have become very clever at being careful. But it has been a bit easier since the Old Professor died and young Willie stepped into his place—literally into his shoes and clothes!"

"Ugh!"

"Just so. But at least we didn't have two of them to watch out for any more."

Mindy glared out from the backless kitchen toward the large feet just visible at the end of the giant bed in the room off the museum. As she did so, they twitched, stretched, and swung unsteadily to the floor.

"Scram!" Her voice was an urgent hiss.

Samantha snatched up the sack and whisked through the swinging door after Mindy. Once in the dark hall she chuckled softly. "I *am* glad you and your Mrs. Bright are here. I won't feel so alone. Golly, I wonder what Miss Britomart would think you meant if you told her to scram! And there are lots of things to do here, you know. Out back of the museum, there's a nice weedy garden. I used to bring in samples of different little seedlings and mosses, until we sorted out which were best to eat. Nurse Morrissey bullies even the Reverend into eating greens."

Coming out the front of the Buckle house onto the walk that was named after Dopple's old Grace Street, the two of them ducked from house to house, keeping close to the imitation shrubbery. They reached the inn without incident, and Samantha led the way to a small side door to which she had a key. Mindy held the sack.

"I wonder if Mrs. Bright's thought up a way to get us out of here yet," Mindy whispered. She watched uncomfortably over her shoulder.

Samantha turned in surprise. Her tone was half mocking and more than half wistful. *"Escape?* Oh, no, Why, the old dears would never allow it."

Eight

"*Escape?* Dear lady, how can you think of it?" The once-young Augustus Dopple wrung his long pale hands. "Only think of the dangers! Field mice as large as lions, mosquitoes as big as blackbirds. And the traffic! Such a rushing and roaring as goes by the museum, why, at the front door the noise itself would knock you flat. And think of your families, your old friends. You are but a little over five inches tall in your world, dear lady. Could they converse with you happily? Or would they not, despite their affection, make a curiosity of you? How could they *not* do so? You would be condemned to a dollhouse life in any case. Here at least you will have companions in misfortune, and though our life is somewhat restricted, our needs are all supplied—after a fashion."

"Well," said Mrs. Bright, blinking, "I didn't

mean only Mindy and myself. And I *did* mean to be unshrunk first."

"I shall never leave," said Miss Umstott in a tragic tone. "The world out there is not my world, not with Mama and Papa gone. I should be utterly alone."

"A pretty woman like yourself?" Mrs. Bright wondered whether she ought to be ashamed, but she felt a positive joy rising at the thought of disconcerting these placid, pasty people. "Why, a month of orange juice and steak and you could find a husband still."

Mr. Goff flicked a furtive glance in Miss Umstott's direction, then sighed heavily and ate another piece of toast.

"And you, Mr. Goff," Mrs. Bright said wickedly. "You must have cut a dashing figure as a young man. I daresay you could again with a little exercise and a lot less toast."

Mr. Goff's nose and cheeks burned, if possible, more brightly. "Used to run cross-country races," he said. He looked sadly at his waistline.

"Vanity, Mrs. Bright, vanity," sorrowed the Reverend Edwards. "No, here we are safe. It is an evil world out there. Bright colors, the frenzy of speed, savage music, loud people with rough and sunburned skins."

"Meaning no offense," Mr. Dopple interjected hastily. "Indeed on Mrs. Bright's cheeks the rosy brown is truly the kiss of the sun." His little bow was both shy and courtly.

"Rough and sunburned," maintained the Reverend, raising his voice to lament, as if to reprove a listening world. "When I was a young man, ladies covered themselves from the sun. Nothing is as it was!"

"And a good thing, too!" Mrs. Bright retorted acidly. "Think how cramped our lives were! And of *course* full-size people sound loud and look awful when you've shrunk to six inches. They must look simply full of pits and wrinkles, I shouldn't wonder. Like the giant Brobdingnagian girl Glumdalclitch in *Gulliver's Travels*. Oh, my dears! Can't you see what has happened? You may be glad to be shut apart from noise and children and change, and sit here complaining at a safe distance. But you are only *ghosts*." Her voice rose in agitation. "Oh, *do* try to be alive! *Want* to get back out into the confusion. I know. Perhaps we cannot. But *want* to. Oh, I *refuse* to be a ghost!" She stamped an angry little foot.

"Hurrah!" Samantha applauded from the doorway, and Mindy slipped in to tuck her hand in Mrs. Bright's.

The Crumps opened the sack of supplies from the Buckle house with exclamations of delight. If out of all the tins even one were good, it would be a treat all around, Jack explained. ("Oh, let it be the pork and beans," he had moaned prayerfully.) It was only with great effort that he managed to tear himself away when Samantha reminded him that he had first watch at the lookout post in the attic now that the Professor was up and stirring. Once Kurtz ate and swept and puttered a while with his machine, he went down into the village, usually returning just before time to open up LILLIPUT U.S.A. at noon.

A bellpull in the attic tower room of the inn, which overlooked the whole of the museum room, rang a small bell in the "keeping room," as the laundry was familiarly called. A single ring repeated at short intervals meant "He's up and about." A double ring meant "all clear," and a continuing ring, as Mrs. Morrissey put it, meant "Freeze or run for your life. He's started dusting over on Grace Street." While Kurtz worked on the houses, everyone remained safely hidden in the keeping room.

"When Jack gives the all clear, I generally head out for the garden," Samantha said.

Miss Umstott spoke graciously. "And I always take a turn along our little High Street and down Grace Street, Mrs. Bright. Perhaps this morning you would care to accompany me? Indeed, I would enjoy seeing the Buckle house, as you call it, again after all these years."

"A-again?"

"Oh yes indeed," said Mr. Dopple. "Your house, dear lady, makes you a charter member of our little family. In the old days it toured with us in the Professor's wagon: PROFESSOR LILLIPUT AND HIS MARVELOUS MUSEUM OF MINIATURES. But before we settled in here, we put in at the Professor's farm for repairs and such. Your house was left behind in the confusion . . ."

". . . and stayed there till I found it!" Mindy forgot for the moment the hunger that had begun to make her stomach rumble. "And that old sign! I found part of the sign that must've been on the wagon. How about that!" It felt very exhilarating to have *something* cleared up, even if it were only the small mystery of PROFESSOR LI and MARVELOUS M.

Mrs. Bright had caught at something else Mr. Dopple said. "What 'confusion'?" she asked.

Mrs. Morrissey shook, jellylike, with amusement at the recollection. "Dear me, but it wasn't half hectic! Turned out 'twasn't his farm at all. The Professor was nothin' but a squatter, and when the rightful owner turned up—after the Great War, that was—why, the sheriff came and turned us off the place. Just as well, I say. Stuck out in that barn we scarce had a thing to eat but greens, and if you don't think *that's* a strain, well!"

"What *do* you eat here? Besides toast, I mean," asked Mindy, after Samantha had warned of the Professor's waking and Jack Crump had put out the fire in the stove that had once served as a laundry boiler and gone off. She eyed the last two pieces of cold toast.

"Oh, cake and breads, rolls, cookies . . . and greens, of course," answered Nurse Morrissey, who looked as if her particular passion was cake. "Once upon a time we tried to make Boston baked beans with columbine seeds and bacon fat, but *real* pork and beans . . ." She eyed the cans hungrily as she explained, "The meat in the Professor's scraps is too coarse, you see, and he always cooks every dribble of broth out of it. So we've had not a morsel of meat for an age. There's milk, though, thanks to Samantha."

Samantha grinned. "I let the milk can down in the firewood basket and go down by rope ladder, then out my own private mousehole. As soon as the milkman's gone, I siphon off what we need."

The silent Sybilla, having poured two steaming cups of coffee and passed the toast to the newcomers, burst out unexpectedly with, "*And* she pinches the flour an' salt an' sugar an' coffee we grind up for ourselves. I ast you fine folks, what're we gonter do when Miss Samantha ain't spry enough to wind the basket up an' down, an' zip up an' down that old rope ladder no more? No more staples, no more milk, no more wood, and no more greens, neither." She shook her head violently, much moved by the prospect of an empty larder.

It was apparent that Samantha's old dears had not thought so far ahead. Now, looking from Samantha to Mindy, it was as if they suddenly felt their lost years very cruelly. And they were afraid. *Would* Samantha have even five years of ladder climbing in her?

"Take heart, dear friends. Do you not see?" The Reverend spoke unctuously, rubbing his hands together, beaming at Mindy. Clearly, he was thinking that she had more than enough ladder-climbing years to take care of them all. "We have been provided for," he said.

Nine

"No!" Samantha's voice was flat and firm as she admonished the oldsters. "You raised me, and I love you all, and up to now I've gone along with whatever you said. But now I think that was wrong. Oh no, not the loving. The going along. Why, you should never have given up! And if Mrs. Bright and Mindy *have* to stay, let's not pretend they *want* to—or that it's *right*."

Nurse Morrissey roused herself, and a faint flush spread over her puffy cheeks. "Oh, if only . . . why, I'd be willing to get seasick swaying down that ladder if there was a real chance. Fudge, I'd *jump* if you had a nice big cushion for me to land on!"

The others stirred, remembering, each one, a different and long-forgotten delight—a place, a season, a favorite food. If only . . .

"Do you know," said Miss Britomart shyly, as if it

were a wicked wish, "I would like to see a motion picture? The Professor's television is too hard on my old eyes—too full of lines—and it growls so. I saw a motion picture once. Robert Harron and Mae Marsh in *The Victim,* it was. So very thrilling!"

"Hey now, I remember that!" Mr. Goff beamed. "It was at the Elysian Picture House over to Mosstown. With Chapter Seven of that serial—*Runaway June,* wasn't it? Always wondered what happened to poor little June." He lapsed back into his melancholy.

The Reverend sighed in pious horror at such worldliness, but if the truth were told, he, too, felt the stirrings of lost delight. He remembered the brief spell during his seminary years when he had supported himself by teaching school. He had been miserable in the job, utterly unsuited for it, but still he remembered the shining children. Clean and dirty, trusting and defiant, they had all been so shining and alive—like candles in the sunshine. He felt a pang as he looked at Mindy and saw that same eager impatience.

"I suppose we have let the light go out," he said sadly.

"Well," said Mindy confidently, "we can fix that. For a start, we ought to figure how to get ourselves unshrunk."

"Dear me! You make it sound so simple," Mrs. Bright teased between sips of coffee. "However," she went on, setting her cup down, "I suppose it *is* just as well to begin with the obvious. Where does Professor Kurtz keep the fatal machine?"

"In a shed outside the back door." Mr. Dopple answered, reaching down a book from the crowded shelves and sketching a precise little plan of the museum on a flyleaf with a stubby pencil. The arrangement was a simple one.

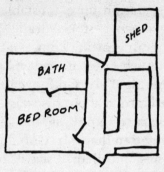

"Ah, you're only wastin' their time, Gus." Mr. Goff wheezed. "We been through all that years ago, Mrs. Bright. It's a monstrous big machine. Big as an icebox and knobs and wires all over. I like to electrocuted myself just trying to flip the *on* switch on the generator. I bet even the Professor don't rightly understand what all them gizmos do. Why, I bet the Old Prof just flang it all together and came up with the Reducer purely by happenstance. The Young Prof works on it like it was a Chinese puzzle. We hear him out there bangin' and cussin' near every blessed morning."

"OK." Mindy was undaunted. "If we can't work it ourselves, at least *he* knows how to work it on houses. We could get somebody to *make* him do it. What's to stop one of us from going out to find a policeman?"

Miss Britomart gasped. "Oh, *promise* you won't do anything so rash! Were you safely to pass the cats next door and reach the corner, you could not cross the street. The wind from passing motorcars is like a hurricane. When we first came to Lake Meander, *I* set out in desperation for a constable and was very nearly blown down a storm drain! I can scarcely think of it without growing faint. And the motorcars drive ever so much faster nowadays." She blushed a little remembering. "Mr. Goff saved me. The other gentlemen tied a rope about his waist, and he swung down from the curb to pull me free of the grating. I have never forgotten that, Mr. Goff."

Mr. Goff's nose purpled. "Pshaw!" he said. "I'd do it again, too, Miss Brit, but they'd never get the rope around me."

Everything, it seemed, had been tried. Every suggestion from Mrs. Bright or Mindy brought a reminiscence: "Do you remember . . ." "Do you recall that nice young man who visited the museum so often in 1930? Samantha went out one day and spoke to him, and he never came back." ("He *fled*," said Samantha. "I think our voices must sound like chipmunk chatter to big folk. I've always wondered if he took me for a skinny dressed-up mouse or a wind-up toy.") Or it was, "No, we tried that in 1932. Or was it '33?" Apparently the only plan left untried was that of sending an explanatory letter to the authorities. But though the Professor kept notepaper in one of the cupboards under the showcase by the front window, he never wrote letters, and so there were neither envelopes nor stamps.

"And," said Mr. Dopple sadly, "the authorities would no doubt dismiss it as an amusing practical joke. Quite understandably."

Glumly Mindy agreed. "I suppose. Like the Chinese fortune-cookie fortune that says, 'Help! I'm a prisoner in a Chinese cookie factory.'" She had begun to be a little discouraged and was not much cheered by Mrs. Bright's homey observation that any knot fingers could tie, fingers could untie.

"I only wish I could let Daddy and Mama know I was here and OK." The tiniest of quavers trembled in her voice.

Mrs. Bright was thoughtful. "Mr. Dopple? Do you have a map? Just how far *are* we from Brittlesdale? I should imagine we were driving for four or five hours last night."

Augustus Dopple reached down a much-thumbed pocket atlas. Mosstown was shown on the Pennsylvania map, but Brittlesdale and Dopple had been too small for inclusion. Mr. Dopple penciled them in.

"But . . . that can't be even a hundred miles!"

"Let me see." Mindy craned to look. "Boy, he must've come by way of every back road in two counties, huh?"

Almost as if it were an answer, a dull, uneven roar from somewhere outside vibrated the room. Mindy and Mrs. Bright jumped up in alarm, but the oldsters scarcely blinked.

"The television." Samantha grinned. "The Prof has the morning news with his porridge and coffee."

"But it sounds so *weird*."

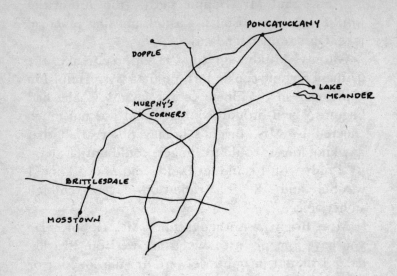

The signal bell rang twice, then once, then three times in a row.

"Come along, honey, and see for yourself." Samantha drew Mindy after her into the hall, explaining as they made their way through the dark labyrinth of hallways and out onto the street. "That tricky little ring on the bells, that's Mr. Crump's signal to me that there's something worth seeing on the television machine. I usually watch from the Umstott's attic. That's the brick house across on Grace Street, next to your Mrs. Bright's house. There's a little window up top set just right for it. My 'box seat,' I call it."

They hurried along High Street and down Grace. As they went, Mindy puzzled over the deep, drawling voice that floated overhead. It was like an imitation of a voice—no, it was like a voice on a record or the radio when the dial was turned all the way down to *bass*.

"Is that because our ears are so little now?" she asked, explaining her thought to Samantha.

"Sounds reasonable." Samantha nodded. "What did you say was opposite of 'bass'? 'Treble'? Well, like I said a bit ago, I always figured we must sound treble-treble—or would, if anybody ever heard us. Sort of like mice and chipmunks used to sound when I was little. I mean, when I was *big*." She laughed ruefully.

In the Umstott attic two old mattresses of blue-and-white ticking filled with straw had been placed against one wall. Mindy found that she could recline very comfortably and, through the gable window across the low dark room, see straight into the professor's living-eating-sleeping room. The television occupied the place of honor on his littered table between the greasy hot plate and a stack of unwashed plates, pots, and cutlery.

"Uhravoonree, bakedascobe," growled the syrupy lady in the commercial. Mindy wriggled down into an almost-flat position and wrinkled her nose and scrunched up her eyes in an effort to sort out what the heavy, vibrating words could mean. Then the familiar face of the Channel Six newscaster loomed beside the steaming coffeepot.

"And now," he said, *"more about last night's mad collector."*

Samantha leaned over, but Mindy signed that she had understood. Out of sight behind the door, the Professor's coffee cup rattled in its saucer. Swinging his slippered feet off the bed, he leaned over to hold the cup over the floor while he poured the spilled coffee back into it from the saucer.

The newscaster was trying to balance his expression between amusement and concern. *"The damage in that explosion in Brittlesdale which leveled Mr. John Hallam's barn was limited to the barn itself; but in addition to the rare and valuable old dollhouse of which no trace was found in the wreckage, we now learn from Officer Edward Beagle of Brittlesdale that the suspected dollhouse thief may have been surprised at his labors by Mrs. William Bright, a neighbor, young Mindy Hallam, owner of the dollhouse, and Horace, the Hallam great Dane. All have been missing since yesterday evening . . ."*

"Horse?" Mindy was puzzled.

". . . and it is now feared there may be a connection between the theft and the disappearances. Police are on the lookout for a blue panel television repair truck and a suspect using the name of L. L. Putt. If you have seen this . . ."

Wilhelm Kurtz clattered his cup down on the table and switched off the announcer in the middle of a word.

"The old lady and the kiddie . . . they couldn't have been!" The worn slippers flapped across the floor, and a rumpled vision in purple and yellow striped pajamas filled the doorway. The Professor scuffed across to the near end of the waist-high table and leaned over to fix a bleary eye on the open bedrooms and kitchen of the Buckle house. Gone was yesterday's dapper look. The face that dipped past the upper Umstott windows was a mass of finely webbed wrinkles. The flesh under his eyes was puffy, and the black hair looked pasted on. Perhaps it was, Mindy thought, faintly surprised.

"Couldn't've been," the Professor repeated. Suddenly he straightened, sucking in his breath and then spitting out the words, *"Mrs. William Bright!* Didn't Uncle's Mary Buckle marry a Bright?"

Samantha pulled Mindy after her into a dark corner of the attic. "You and Mrs. B. didn't move anything upstairs, did you?" The question seemed to shape itself inside Mindy's ear, it was so soft a whisper. "You didn't leave anything lying around that could give you away?"

"No. No, I don't think so. Anyhow, there was stuff on the floor all over the house. And we didn't have anything with us, only our clothes."

"The beds. Did you sleep in one of the beds?"

"I spread it up and put the nighties under the pillow. Oh, what's he doing now?"

"Mmm . . . can't see. He's over on the front-door side. Come along. We'd better take cover."

They tiptoed to the stairwell and down. As they slipped along the upstairs hall, the slapping footsteps could be heard moving away and a moment later hurrying back. Breathless, Samantha and Mindy reached the ground floor and the cupboard beneath the stairs. Once safely inside, Samantha lit a candle. "A hidey-hole in every house," she said. Across the top of the door, holes had been drilled for ventilation, and tucked inside the roomy cupboard were a small easy chair, a low cot, an orange-crate bookshelf with books, and a supply of short, stumpy candles.

"We make them ourselves." Samantha set the flickering candle in a saucer. "Ever since we used up the last of the candles and lamp oil in the Emporium. The Prof doesn't miss the occasional candle end."

Mindy winced at the noises and loud grumbling that came to them from next door. "Golly, I hope he doesn't notice how the drapes in the dining room are pinned together. Oh, Samantha, do we *have* to stay shut up in here?"

Samantha was torn. She had been brought up to take cover at the least sign of danger, and if to her that had seemed sometimes cowardly, it was after all a question of surviving. The Professor was very large and very spiteful.

Mindy bounced impatiently on the cot. "How can we know what to do if we don't watch to see what he knows?"

Samantha agreed to leave the hidey-hole, and they watched from the Umstott parlor. The Professor, having forced a window in the Buckle dining room, lifted the drapes with a finger and peered in. He missed seeing that the brocade was pinned together, for something else caught his eye. With a long pair of tweezers he reached in and brought out a curious collection of articles, which he lined up on the painted front lawn: a kitchen candlestick, a book in a green cover, and two plates, each with a cellophane candy wrapper crumpled in the middle.

Ten

Mindy could almost see the wheels turning in his mind. Why should these things have been so neatly placed on the table when everything else in the house that was not fastened down was on the floor? Yet, would anyone sit reading by candlelight in a house that had been carted away in a van? Had the book and candle perhaps been there—how long had it been?—forty-eight years ago? He pulled nervously at his little moustache, trying desperately to remember. Nothing must happen now. Not now, his anxiety seemed to say. Any day—today perhaps—he would have the answer to that little problem of the field sensor (or the magnetic compensator—perhaps that was the trouble). To be so close to triumph . . .

The Professor squinted at the tiny shreds of cellophane gripped in his tweezers. What could they mean? Why neatly placed on a plate? He gave a sigh

of helpless bewilderment, and before he could cup his hand to catch them, the tiny scraps blew away and twinkled down to the dusty floor.

The Professor padded into the other room for a tissue and blew his nose so vigorously that when he returned to contemplate the Buckle house, his head seemed clear of worry as well. He beamed. "Ha, should have thought of it before," he said aloud. "Of course. No dog here. Couldn't be. The beast came for me *after* I turned the Reducer from *Magnify* to *Minify*. Saw him in the rear-view mirror, too, that first half-mile or so."

He grinned. "Bet the old lady trundled out her little jalopy, and she and the kid tried to follow, too. Led 'em a dizzy chase, I did. Nobody catches old Kurtz!" He chortled. "Oh, you beautiful machine. Thought they'd hide the old house from me, didn't they? But Kurtz was too sharp for 'em. I would've known them bits of dinky furniture in the shop window even if I hadn't gotten wind of there bein' an auction there. Nosirree, house, they couldn't hide you from my Reducer! Once I guessed where they'd tucked you away, one flip of m' new magnification switch and up you came, barn or no, big as life. Too risky for me to break in—them windows was too high up. I'd've broke a leg for sure. But that don't stop old Kurtz. Mebbe I can't break in, but the house surely could break out!"

Mindy's eyes widened. "Why, he broke our barn down on *purpose*," she hissed in Samantha's ear.

Samantha put a finger to her lips in warning and nodded toward the window. The Professor had leaned quite close, and they could feel the vibration as his fingers drummed on the long table.

He chuckled. "Yessirree-bob! Flip the switch over to *Minify* and down you went," he crooned to the Buckle house. "With nary a soul the wiser. I *knew* the old Reducer could magnify what it had reduced! Simple logic! Must've been the wiring on the old switch that kept you from working in reverse before. Never give up! Trial and error! Ho, ho!" He patted the Buckle house on the roof and danced a little shuffle out the back door to the Reducer's shed.

"How fortunate that you did not leave any clearer traces of your presence!" Miss Britomart fanned herself violently with a palm-leaf fan bearing the legend VISIT ATLANTIC CITY. "We would have been forced into an exceedingly unpleasant situation."

Mrs. Bright's eyebrows went up inquiringly.

"Well, um, yes, dear lady," said Mr. Dopple. He looked as if he were about to fall down in a fit of timidity and mortification. "You *do* see, don't you," he quavered, "that he would still have no intimation of our presence? We should have to t-trust to your magnanimity."

Mindy understood his tone sufficiently to understand the little speech without knowing precisely what "magnanimity" might mean. She stared unbelievingly around the circle of timorous oldsters gathered in the entrance hallway of the inn. Fearful and tenacious. They meant to keep to their little kingdom until they shriveled, no matter what. They meant that Mrs. Bright and Mindy would have to go out and give themselves up. It was an angry Samantha who broke the uncomfortable silence. "You should all be ashamed! Don't you worry, Mrs. Bright. You and Mindy have some backbone left, though I can think of some for whom I can't say the same. Don't you give in!" She spoke bravely, but was clearly worried. "We'll think of *some*thing."

They had not thought of a thing by the time the Professor slammed through the front door of the museum at ten-thirty, fully an hour before his usual return from the village. He had the look of a small thundercloud ready to spit lightning and rumble furiously at the slightest prod. In an angry rush he hurled the late morning final of the *Mosstown Monitor* on the floor, fastened the CLOSED TODAY sign on the front door, drew down all the blinds, and switched on the electric lights. Had he been in a little less of a fury, he might have seen Samantha, Mindy, Mrs. Bright, and a completely terrified Jack and Sybilla Crump caught in the open. In the "vacant lot" at the far corner of the table, between the inn and the general store, the Emporium, the usual morning foray for supplies became a wild scramble. Halfway across to the far corner table leg, Mindy and Samantha had a knobbly gunnysack of percolator-ground coffee, a bucket of coarse flour, and a small bundle of dry firewood. The rope ladder dangled down along the side and in the shadow of a table leg. The arrangement was convenient not only because the ladder was sheltered from view, but also because it was quite handy to the inn. And being so near the inn, it was a constant worry to the inn's occupants, even though ladders, baskets, and ropes were carefully stowed away when not in use. The Professor's untimely return had sent the whole of Dopple into a panic.

After an angry tongue-lashing from Mrs. Bright, only the Crumps had been persuaded to come out and lend a hand at the winch. While Mindy climbed, Mrs. Bright suggested, Samantha could ride up in the large basket. "I *couldn't* very well do it all by myself," she wheezed, as she and Mr. Crump cranked away at the winch years earlier improvised for hauling up large loads. Looking over her shoulder, she gasped. "Oh, do have a care, Mrs. Crump!"

The small supply bucket was swaying upward toward the edge of the table. Sybilla stood at a window on the inn's side porch, feet planted against the window seat, and she hauled at the rope hand over hand. The bucket lurched up, an inch at a time, an unsteady progress that stalled as the bucket came to an abrupt stop under the edge of the table.

"Oh, dear! It's stuck. Whatever shall I do?" poor Sybilla moaned, casting frantic glances around the floor and over the porch ceiling, as if help might come out of the woodwork. She was too nearsighted to make out what had gone wrong.

"Hold on, old girl. You're doin' just fine. But you hold on a minnit just like you are." Mr. Crump puffed the words out in a windy whisper from the spot near the Emporium's side door where he and Mrs. Bright cranked away at the rope that was bringing Samantha up in the inn's large wicker laundry basket. "Just you hold still till we get little Samantha up, honey," he said. "Any of that coffee and firewood goes on the floor, we're in for it."

Sybilla tried to tie the rope to a nearby table leg, but her old fingers seemed all thumbs, and twice she tied one of them into the fumbled knot.

"Drat!" she muttered. "Danged if I don't think Mrs. Bright has the right of it. It's eyeglasses I need, an' somethin' for my poor stiff joints."

She was almost in tears when Mr. Goff sidled

through the inner doorway to tiptoe up behind her like a timid elephant. Patting her awkwardly on the shoulder, he said, "You hang on there, Syb," in a whispery croak. He eased out the side door with a surprising agility and a rediscovered courage that surprised no one so much as himself. He headed for the bucket.

As Samantha and the basket came up to table level, she was greeted by an astonishing spectacle. Across the rooftops she saw the top of the Professor's head as he banged out the back door and into the shed. In the angle between the Lilliput Inn and the Emporium—in full sight, had he turned to look— the dignified Miss Umstoff trotted across the grass-green table with a load of firewood cradled in her hiked-up skirts. Sybilla came after with the basket of coffee, and Mr. Goff, looking alarmingly like a large bundle of blue blankets about to roll over the edge, was letting the bucket down to Mindy for the pail of flour and the rest of the firewood. The big laundry basket passed it on the way down, and with Samantha at the winch, Mindy and the last of the supplies made a neck-and-neck race of it on the way back up. At the same time Mr. Dopple hauled up the rope ladder and lugged it to its hiding place under the window seat on the inn porch. He was back to steady the basket when it bumped against the table and swayed perilously, and to give Mindy a hand out.

Not a moment too soon. A large handkerchief flapped in the attic window where Mrs. Morrissey kept watch. The Professor was already at the back door. Mindy and Mr. Goff were the last to reach cover, Mindy dragging the large basket after her into the store and Herman Goff pushing shut the trapdoor in the side wall of the Emporium. The sturdy little winch disappeared into the wall as the panel closed. Inside, Mr. Crump shot the trapdoor bolts home. Mindy held the door open, and Mr. Goff lumbered through it.

"Gus'll have the ladies safe in the keeping room," Mr. Goff said when he had caught his breath. "So we're all accounted for but the Reverend."

"Aye. Surprised me, the Reverend did." Jack Crump wheeled a small fire screen marked $4.95 around to hide the winch, now inside, from the large front windows of the store.

Mindy's attention veered from the fascinating shelves of Phoenix Silk Hose (75¢), One-Button Union Suits ($1), and Hallmark Shirts ($1 and up), with tabs for fastening on fresh collars (two for 25¢). "Why? Where *is* the Reverend?"

Old Herman Goff shook his head in wonder. "Never thought I'd see it. Never thought I'd see the Reverend let loose of his dignity. I tell you, little lady, it did my heart good to see him harin' across the back way to the church, coattails all a-flap. And brave as he was spry! Meant to raise a distraction if we needed it. Play the organ or ring the church bells, I reckon. Eada would've signaled him from up where she is. Gosh, Jack," he said, a note of worry creeping into his voice, "I hope the old duffer made it back safe."

But Mr. Crump's alarm was directed elsewhere. "Herman, you get outa that swivel chair and down behind them iceboxes! The Professor's just hove in sight." His moustache fairly bristled. "You, little girl! Mindy? Mindy. Mindy, what say you scamper yourself up to that front window there and see what the old buzzard's up to? Me, I'm too creaky to keep low enough to the floor. Now, take care you keep down, hear?" He watched her edge away. "I *would* go if I wasn't too stiff to hunker down thataway," he said in wistful apology to Mr. Goff.

Mindy crept along between the toothpastes, soaps, and sundries and the bicycle pumps, air guns, and vacuum jugs, then made a dash across the open end aisle to shelter below the display rack of cigarettes (Fatimas, 15¢) and the magazine rack. Far away, down at the end of the long, open U of the table the town was perched on, she could see where Kurtz had set up a small worktable. As she watched, he picked up the Buckle house, hoisted it across to the smaller table, and began systematically to remove its furnishings, all the while muttering angrily to himself. He forced windows, tweezed open wardrobe doors, and in fact did everything but turn the house over and shake it. Fortunately he was so angrily intent upon his work that he did not once look up, or he might have seen three faces watching avidly from the Emporium window, for Mr. Goff and Mr. Crump had found curiosity stronger than caution. It was Mr. Goff who guessed the Professor's intention.

"By jingo, he *does* know you and Mrs. Bright are here, Mindy girl. I think the old devil means to isolate every house an' give it a going-over till he finds you. He'll figure you're bound to turn up in the last one, if not before. Why, the old . . . ! Lookit there!"

Kurtz had opened the cupboard beneath the museum's front window display cases and, after rummaging among his cleaning materials, had selected a half-full plastic spray bottle and a squat green plastic jug. He unscrewed the spray top, set the bottle on the table, and filled it up from the other container. WINDO-KLEER said the spray bottle: *With More Ammonia.* The green jug was straight ammonia.

"He's looking awful mean," said Mindy, nervously chewing at a fingernail. "He *looks* like somebody who'd torment kittens."

"I don't like it at all." Mr. Crump chewed at his faded red moustache while the Professor calmly began spraying a fine mist in through the windows of the Buckle house. "Why, one whiff o' that stuff, and a body couldn't help givin' himself away with coughin'. Set you to weepin' for hours, it can, once you get it in your eyes."

Mr. Goff, forgetful where he was, raised up to his full six inches and swelled with indignation. "Why, why . . . the villain!" He straightened his baggy jacket with sudden decision and said firmly, "Come!" He was splotchy with emotion—even his bald head was red—and, to Mindy's way of thinking, very splendid. She followed obediently down the paint and hardware aisle, out the side door, and into the inn, Mr. Crump following after.

"There. *That's* what set him going," said Mrs. Bright. She pointed down from the window to the museum floor and handed Samantha's field glasses to Mr. Goff.

Everyone was crowded into the attic of the inn—everyone except the Reverend Edwards. With Kurtz working no more than three feet away from the church, there was considerable concern for the Reverend's safety. Mr. Dopple and Mr. Crump had resolved to go after him if he were not back within ten minutes.

Mrs. Morrissey fretted. "I gave an all clear wave, but he didn't signal back."

"Well, I swan!" exclaimed Mr. Goff. He passed the binoculars to Mindy and pointed to the newspaper that the Professor had thrown on the floor.

It was the *Mosstown Monitor*. In the middle of the front page, under the heading "Horace on the Trail," a rather muddled paragraph described the baffling occurrences in Brittlesdale. The following paragraph read:

> . . . But help is on the way! Early this morning news came from Murphy's Corners that Horace, the great Dane, supposed last night to have been among the abducted, passed through that mountain hamlet shortly after dawn. Murphy's Corners is forty miles north of Brittlesdale. Mr. John Hallam, father of the missing Mindy, believes that the dog is on the trail of his young mistress. Officer Edward Beagle reports that "Old Horace has a darned good nose." State and local police are now on the lookout for the dog . . .

"North?" said Mindy. "Good old Horse! But why's he going straight north?"

Mrs. Bright figured rapidly in her mind. How many miles could a dog cover in an hour? "He'll be following all that roundabout way we took, dear. He can't *possibly* get here before tonight. And the trail will be growing fainter all the while . . ."

Brrmgandnow . . .

The Professor had switched on a battered little transistor radio. "*. . . for the eleven o'clock news. Horace, that great Dane we've been hearing so much about, has now passed through Benmawr, crossing U.S. 30 and heading south. State police report that from time to time the dog ranges across and away* *from the road, as if trying to catch a scent laid down at high speed. Persons sighting the dog are requested not to interfere in any way."*

"Blast!" The Professor switched off the radio. Hurriedly returning the last of the furniture to the Buckle kitchen, he hoisted the house up and deposited it on the floor in the far corner of the room.

Miss Britomart's handkerchief flew to her mouth. She gave a little moan of distress, thinking the Umstott house was to be next. "All that lovely William Morris wallpaper," she whispered. "The spray will simply ruin it!"

But it was not the Umstott house that Kurtz swung up and over onto the smaller table. It was the church. The little company in the attic exchanged horrified looks.

"The Reverend!"

Eleven

"No, no, *quite* all right." The Reverend held up a hand to quiet the babel of questions. His face was scratched, he was red-eyed, and his wispy hair stood up in a raggedy white halo, but he seemed to have taken no serious damage.

"A sixth sense warned, or I should never have left the bell tower when I did, dear friends. I tremble to think what the consequences would have been. I was fortunate indeed. I leaped out the vestry door into a clump of sponge-rubber shrubbery in the very nick of time."

He had remained in the shrubbery, considerably shaken, for the better part of an hour. Only after the noon news, when Horace was reported trotting through Sorley Summit, and the Professor had slammed out the front door and set out in the blue van with a great grinding of gears, had the Reverend been able to summon the strength to hail the search party that gathered in despair at the table's edge to halloo the church where it sat on the museum floor. Now he sat enjoying a mug of hot milk and a comfortable chair in the keeping room, and seemed as much excited as exhausted.

"Sorley Summit, you say? That is *much* closer, is it not? A courageous and intelligent beast, your Horace." The Reverend raised his glass of milk to Mindy in a salute that seemed positively light-hearted.

Sorley Summit was much closer. Mr. Dopple had drawn up a map of the immediate area on a sheet of butcher paper from the Emporium, copying the old

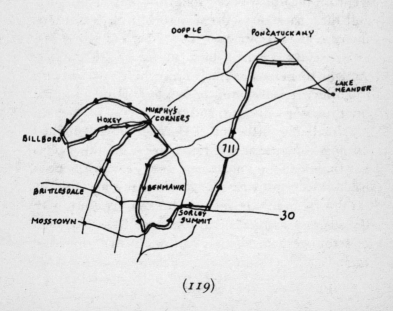

highway routes from the atlas and filling in from memory connecting roads and precise locations of the villages and hamlets where Horace had been sighted. The Professor's route to Lake Meander had been devious to the point of silliness.

Mrs. Bright tapped a thoughtful finger against her chin. "I could have *sworn* we were in Hoxey at one point. That dreadful clatter tires make on the metal grid of the bridge, you know? I'm sure that's what wakened me at one point."

"Hoxey? I do believe the Professor said something about Hoxey as he slammed out the front door." The Reverend snapped his fingers impatiently, trying to remember. "Something about 'skipping Hoxey.'"

Mindy traced the route on the map with her finger, then looked up with a delighted grin. "If we went round this way to Hoxey, by way of Billboro, and then back the short way to Murphy's Corners, then we crossed our own trail. I bet old Horse just followed the freshest one out of the Corners— straight to Benmawr, then down here and back up to Sorley. It makes him *miles* closer. Do you s'pose the Professor's given up and run away?"

"Not likely, little lady," Herman Goff drummed his fingers on the arm of his chair. "Too full of plots not to be hatching out a new one. Let's just hope it backfires and your Horace gets here in time with the cavalry. Mmm. No danger of his coming down with the staggers, is there? Sensible dog? Knows enough to scrounge a meal and take a breather now and again?"

"Oh, yes." Mindy nodded positively. "If only we can keep out of the Professor's way long enough, Horse'll be here. No matter what." She was struck by a sudden thought. "*I* know! Why not let the Professor think we got away? Mrs. Bright and me, I mean. We could take the rope off the little supply bucket—not the rope ladder, because he'd know it took a long time to make. Anyhow, we could take the rope and hang it down to the floor over on the corner near the back door! Like we'd gone out that way?"

"An excellent idea, dear child!" Miss Umstott leaned over to give Mindy an impulsive little kiss. She smelled of lavender and musty cupboards. All of the oldsters were surprised and admiring. Their surprise seemed to say that such constructive thinking from one of so few and tender years was something altogether unexpected. Mindy was a little uncomfortable under their praise. In their little tabletop world did the old saying, "Children should be seen and not heard," mean that children were supposed to keep their heads empty?

Everyone smiled fondly, and Miss Britomart pressed Mindy to take a cookie from the plate Sybilla had filled fresh from the oven. Mr. Crump poured glasses of milk for everyone, and the little company relaxed back into their chairs.

"Them cookies is lunch," Sybilla snapped. "Share 'em around. No greens today. And if you want to know what *I* think, *which* nobody never does, *I* think folks who'd loll around waitin' for a dog to rescue 'em are sillier than sheep. Sheep an' chickens."

Blamed silly animals." She stumped back to the stove and proceeded to ignore them all.

There was an uncomfortable pause. It was Mrs. Bright who spoke first, tilting her head with her little birdlike gesture. "Mrs. Crump is absolutely right. Yes, Why, as Mr. Goff says, we haven't a notion what young Willie Kurtz may be up to. And we ought not count on dear Horace to keep up the splendid pace he has managed so far. The trail must be very faint indeed by now. We must be realistic. We can count on no one but ourselves."

The others grew very serious over their milk and cookies.

"Bravely said, little lady." Augustus Dopple sighed. "But habit is strong. We have not had such a morning as this these fifty years! And yet we would at the least excuse slide back into our hiding and waiting. I do not blame our good Sybilla for her sharp tongue. We have indeed become sheep and chickens."

"Here now, here now!" Mr. Goff objected. "Let's not get in a swivet. Let's ask, 'What's to do?' Little Mindy's given us the first step. Now: any more ideas? What about you, ma'am?" He turned back to Mrs. Bright.

She hesitated. "Didn't you say that Lilliput U.S.A. was Professor Kurtz's only income? Now that cannot be very much, can it? There must be very few visitors in the winter months. I was thinking— what would he do if he suddenly saw a way to get a great deal of money all at once?"

Jack Crump laughed. "Why, the poor bird'd fall

over his own feet goin' after it. Likely he'd chuck the museum and work on that dad-burned machine twenty-five hours a day."

"Good!" Mrs. Bright had a gleam in her eye. She cocked her head quizzically. "Then perhaps you can tell me, Mr. Dopple, why the original Professor Wilhelm Kurtz did not simply *unshrink* your bank and, shall we say, 'make a withdrawal?' "

Mr. Dopple blinked. "Great Scott! Dear me, I don't know," he said blankly. "How very peculiar. Indeed, how *very* peculiar. Do you know, the possibility never occurred to me? But . . . *bank robbery?* Would he be so audacious as to rob a bank?" Clearly it was a new and shocking idea to Mr. Dopple.

Old Jack Crump cackled. "You're a one, Gus! Why, he stole the *bank*. Why not the money?"

"Just like the old bungler, ain't it?" Herman Goff hooted with laughter. "Right under his nose all these years! And him pinchin' pennies all the while so hard you could hear 'em squeal."

Augustus Dopple recovered from his amazement. "Actually, there was not all that much cash in the bank on that Saturday in 1915. We had many withdrawals on the Friday—farmers off to the County Fair with an eye to buying new stock, and the townfolk meaning to make it a real holiday. They left only a few hundreds in the vault, and the bank messengers were due the next Monday with more cash. Quite possibly Kurtz had known this."

"Ah, that is not so good." Mrs. Bright nibbled pensively at a cookie. "I had thought we might somehow tempt this Willie to unshrink the bank."

"With us in it!" Mindy burst out with the thought that drew everyone to the edges of their chairs.

Samantha clapped her hands in delight. "And we could lure him into the vault room and shut him in!"

Mr. Dopple's faded eyes lit up. "Quite improper. Not at all fitting to a bank's dignity. But it might just work! If only he does not know how low our funds are."

Miss Britomart leaned across the corner of the table and gave a gentle pull at Mr. Dopple's coat sleeve. "Augustus? I don't know that it would help, but . . . what about the securities in my papa's safe-deposit box?"

Mr. Dopple patted her hand kindly. "It is very good of you to try to help, my dear, but that is impossible. It would take your papa's key and his signature to open his box."

"But, Augustus. Papa must have passed away simply *years* ago. The securities would be mine now. The key must be over in Papa's desk. I could—"

Mr. Dopple was distressed. "But the formalities . . ."

"Mr. Dopple!" Mindy slid down in her chair, overcome by giggles.

Augustus Dopple flushed, straightening primly. But then a smile twitched at his mouth. "Habits of a lifetime," he murmured. Then he spoke firmly. "When Dopple is returned to Dopple, I must have a sign made to place above my desk: FLEXIBILITY. A very good word, I begin to see. Flexibility is strength. What is rigid is more surely frangible.

What is—" With an embarrassed little cough he recollected himself and turned back to the problem at hand. "Very well, Miss Brit. Do you know what securities Mr. Umstott held?"

"Ten thousand shares of something-or-other," she answered vaguely.

"*Something*-or-other? Hm. Something-or-other."

All of the gentlemen smiled affectionately at Miss Britomart, who blushed and dropped her eyes. "I don't really understand such things," she murmured.

Mr. Goff harumphed and looked sentimental.

"*Indelible Typewriter Ribbon Company?*"

"Indelible Typewriter Ribbon Company. Ten thousand shares." Mr. Dopple riffled through the sheaf of securities and observed sadly, "Five cents a share, if I recall correctly. Not a very tempting sum. *If* Indelible typewriter ribbons are made at all nowadays."

"I never heard of them," Mindy volunteered, craning to see. But in a moment she and the others had swiveled around in surprise. Mrs. Bright was dancing a little jig in the middle of the outer vault room.

"Oh, my dears! He will never be able to resist it. Oh, it is too, too perfect! *My* papa gave me twenty-five cents' worth of Indelible Typewriter Ribbon shares when I was twelve. His little birthday joke, he said. He would have been astonished had he known that those shares would come to provide a considerable part of my income!" She laughed at their looks of blank surprise. "You see, my dears, *Indelible* was one of the parent companies that became M.B.M.—Mammoth Business Machines!"

Mindy's eyes widened, but apparently the worldwide fame of that giant corporation had not extended to Dopple. The name meant nothing to the oldsters.

Mrs. Bright calculated rapidly in her head. "Ten thousand shares. With the stock divisions and reinvested dividends, that would be . . ." She eyed Samantha and the old ladies and gentlemen mischievously. "It comes to something in the neighborhood of a million dollars."

Everyone was tongue-tied with amazement. The only sound was a small wordless croak from Sybilla Crump.

Mr. Goff regarded Mrs. Bright somberly and mopped his bald head with a large handkerchief. Finding his voice at last, he wheezed, "Boy, oh!" After gathering his wits together with an effort, he turned to the others with a gusty sigh. "Well, well! OK. Let's shake a leg, then. Somebody fetch Mrs. Morrissey along down from the attic at the inn. We'd best set up housekeepin' here in the bank. And we'll have to figger a way to mousetrap the Prof."

Once a plan was settled on, everyone scurried. Mrs. Morrissey came bustling back with Mr. Crump only a minute before the Professor's key was heard in the back door. Samantha, posted as lookout in the cupola atop the bank, saw the door flung open and reported that the truck parked at the back was a large U-Haul-It, and not the Professor's own blue van. This news caused considerable confusion in the bank and considerable rush in the Emporium, where Mindy and Miss Britomart were at work with a large piece of tag board, brushes, and a pot of ink made up from the Emporium's small stock of ink and a bottle of *Mrs. Tuttle's Laundry Bluing*.

"Dear me," gravely pronounced the formal Miss Brit as she wiped up a small blot with the hem of her long skirt. "I suppose this is what nowadays you call The Big Crunch? I *do* hope *we* shan't be crunched."

Twelve

Willie Kurtz's back ached. Much as it made him wince to admit it, he was not as young as he used to be. Time was, years ago, he could have hoisted his Lilliput Inn up easy as a whistle, lugged it to the truck, and have it stowed quick as a wink. Now he was stretched out on the bed with the heating pad switched up to *hot* under the small of his back, and the television turned on for Channel Six news. While the weatherman moved clouds and rainstorms around his map, Willie Kurtz debated whether he could safely ask his next-door neighbor, the Souvenir Shoppe man, to give him a hand with loading the Reducer. But how would he explain moving the whole of Lilliput U.S.A. away from Lake Meander before the peak of the tourist season? Moreover, the neighbors might already be putting two and two together what with all this jabber about missing dollhouses and that dad-blamed dog jogging closer every minute.

On the television the newscaster looked up from his script with a smile. *"Well, our canine friend Horace Hallam is still at it. After a steak furnished by a Summit County sheriff's deputy and an hour's siesta this afternoon, Horace was back on the trail of the suspected kidnapper. It now seems probable that the name used by the suspect—L. L. Putt—was an alias. There is no trace of any such person owning or operating an electronics and television repair service in Pennsylvania, West Virginia, or Maryland. Police admit that, at the moment, Horace is their only lead. So his owner, Mr. John Hallam, says, 'We can only hope that Horace and the trail hold out.' The last report from the patrol car following the large great Dane is that he is now on Route 711 and could be heading for either Poncatuckany or Lake Meander . . ."*

The Professor gave a dreadful groan, switched off the heating pad, and lurched up to switch off the distressing news. "All my life's work and Uncle's!" He moaned. "Risked for a stupid house. Ah, if only I had left it well enough alone in Brittlesdale! They would have gone on supposing it no more than a dollhouse. No reason to think otherwise, was there? A nervous old fool, that's what I am." He reached for the coffeepot. "Poncatuckany? Wisht I *had* gone through Poncatuckany. The smell from the paper mill'd have covered the trail like a blanket."

But flight was now the only answer. Far away. He would go to New Jersey. No, not far enough. Florida? All the work of setting the museum up in a new location—the very thought made him weary. And he had been *so* close to perfecting the Reducer. Fifty dollars. Only fifty dollars more, and he could make a set of magnetic. . . . The thought trailed off as he found himself staring fixedly at something that should not have been where it was.

A string hung from the corner of the great U-shaped table in the museum room. Odd. Odd that he should not have noticed it when he had carried the town hall out to the truck. He poured a cup of reheated coffee and went out to take a look. It was not a string. It was a tiny rope, tied to the dowel-rod trunk of a dusty imitation tree, and knotted at intervals. The bottom end brushed the floor.

"By the great Harry!" The professor gaped. "They *was* here. And gone! But where in blazes could they go? Blast that Mary Bright, she's the bad luck of the Kurtzes, she is. *And* the brat she's got with her."

The back door, he noticed, was ajar. They could be well away by now. He tried to think what difference this new development made, but his mind moved as stickily and slowly as molasses. No Florida now. That was clear. If Mary Bright and the brat found help, Pago Pago would not be far enough away from Lilliput U.S.A. He knelt, fingering the rope, filled with confusion, unseeing eyes fixed on the dusty floor. It was minutes before, rousing himself, the Professor saw the scrap of paper a scant three feet away.

Creaking forward onto his knees under the table, Kurtz picked it up and turned it over, idly, blankly.

Then suddenly eyes and mind sharpened, and he teetered sideways unsteadily. Fumbling, all thumbs, he smoothed it flat against his knee. A flimsy scrap of cream colored notepaper, it was only three inches wide and was torn across the bottom. Jotted on it—apparently in haste and with a leaky pen—was a cryptic memo.

> *Dopple? disap 1915?*
> *Chk newspprs re: lost*
> *fortune in securities*
> *in D. bnk. Ask U.*
> *Wrnt they Indel. Typewr?*
> *now M B M?*

Kurtz forgot that he was under the table. Rising up in his excitement, he fetched himself a smart crack on his head, which was already reeling. A fortune? The lovely word rang like a peal of bells. *D. bnk?* Dopple Bank. *His* bank. It *had* to mean that. He felt a sudden, damping chill. Someone knew, then, about Dopple. Who could have dropped the note? Had the room been swept since closing time on Saturday? He thought not. Saturday. That had to be it. But there had been dozens of visitors on Saturday, and none had seemed overly curious. Unless . . . no, it could *not* be a ruse—that was sure—for meddling Mary Buckle Bright could have no knowledge of what was locked up in the bank. No, it had been someone with some connection with Dopple. *Ask U.* Ask Umstott? No, the Miss Britomart Uncle had courted had been an only child, and if she had married, her children would not be Umstotts. Could it be a nephew? A cousin? The Professor's hand shook and panic rose. If discovery was closing in from both sides, there was no time to lose. All of the houses— all except the bank—were already in the truck. The bank and the Reducer must be loaded and moved at once.

Only then did the light dawn. A fortune in the bank. A fortune in negotiable securities. Who needed Lilliput U.S.A.?

Backache forgotten, the Professor rushed into preparations for possessing himself of the fortune so happily close at hand. Having rooted an old wheelbarrow out of the shed, he tooled it through the back door and around into the well of the U-shaped table where the bank sat, looking deceptively blank and rather shabby. Hoisting it up, Kurtz transferred it to the handbarrow with a jarring *thunk,* and wheeled it out of doors at a trot, down the weedy graveled path to the field beyond the bottom of the tangled garden. In the middle of a largish space, well screened from the neighbors by trees, he unloaded it hurriedly onto the grass and trotted back up the path to fetch the Reducer. A large and ungainly machine, it had been fitted with grip handles and caster wheels for ease in movement. In a moment it was rattling down the uneven path, the Professor fairly flying behind. Only luck, in the shape of a chance encounter of a small front wheel with a large pine cone, kept machine and professor from plunging past the bank and into the small stream that trickled across the field's far edge.

The Professor, straining hard, with grunts and

wheezes, lined the Reducer up with the bank, where it sat cupola-high in the weeds. He aimed it carefully. The focusing apparatus was screwed in and out until he was satisfied with its adjustment. To the watchers in the bank it looked, more than anything else, like a large and comical pig-snout wound around with wire like an electrical coil.

"Think the old geezer knows what he's doin'?" Herman Goff breathed in Augustus Dopple's ear.

"I most sincerely hope so." Mr. Dopple put a hand on his stomach, as if to calm the flutter that was growing more violent with every suspenseful minute. Carefully, on tiptoe, the two old men moved away from the front window, where they had watched through the clear glass letters that spelled out FIRST BANK on the frosted glass window. The words OF DOPPLE had long ago been pasted over with an old Christmas sticker on which the Professor had neatly lettered JOIN OUR CHRISTMAS CLUB.

The others were already out of sight, and at Mr. Goff's signal deep breaths were taken all around. This was, as Miss Britomart had put it, the Big Crunch. The Professor had followed their lure and was about to bite. The bank's front door was helpfully unlocked and the outer vault room door accommodatingly ajar. The combination to the vault was conveniently noted on a slip of paper clipped to a bulletin board hanging beside the vault door.

The waiting and the silence became increasingly uncomfortable. Sybilla struggled with a hay-feverish urge to sneeze. Mindy uncrossed and recrossed her fingers, shifting her weight from one heel to the other as she crouched out of sight behind a filing

cabinet in the outer vault room. After several uncomfortable moments, Mrs. Bright slipped from her
hiding place and crept up the rickety stairs to join
Samantha in the cupola. Torn between her determi-
nation to have things restored to their proper proportions and her reluctance to watch poor old Willie
Kurtz's nephew make his last blunder, she had decided that she did not care to be near the vault room
when the trap was sprung.

Still nothing happened. The Reducer hummed
and thrummed. A cool evening breeze ruffled the
crabgrass and ragweed. But nothing happened.

"Oh, oh, oh!" The Professor danced excitedly
around the machine, flipping switches and making
adjustments according to the readings on the confus-
ing profusion of dials. This involved further delay,
as he had to fetch paper and pencil in order to make
the necessary calculations. At last he drew a deep
breath and moved the main switch from *Inactive* to
Magnify. Nervously, he peered out from behind the
Reducer. The bank had not grown an inch.

The Professor's dark head bobbed up and down
behind the machine in a frenzy of adjustments and
impatience. Mrs. Bright and Samantha, watching
from the cupola window, saw his growing agitation
with mixed approval and distress. With a fortune
near enough to touch, but yet out of reach, he was
suffering from a rising fever of greed. Elbows, flap-
ping coattails, little moans of anticipation and
frustration—everything about him quivered with
avarice. Further adjustment. Surely . . .

But nothing happened at all.

Thirteen

"Where do you s'pose we are now?"

Mindy spoke sleepily from the corner where she sat curled up between soft, cushiony Mrs. Bright and the bony, more angular Samantha. The bank jiggled and swayed as the large truck rumbled through the evening, and it was difficult to catch more than a blink or two of sleep. The oldsters were awake, but no one answered. Exhaustion and disappointment had left them withdrawn, almost uncaring.

Samantha frowned at the silence, which was not so much directed at Mindy's question nor at the cruel chance of having seen their hopes dashed, as at what they conceived to have been the cruel raising of those hopes in the first place. "Never you mind, child," Samantha said with a pointed glance around the bank manager's office, where the company had gathered. "It was an excellent idea. And if it didn't work, why there's no one *here* to blame."

"No, indeed," seconded Mrs. Bright firmly. "I say, better a good try that fizzles out than no try at all."

"Mmjoh. Must keep a hand in. Never despair. *Spes vita est*," announced the Reverend, rallying somewhat. "Dear friends, let us not wallow in this Slough of Despond."

"Stupid old machine, anyway." Mindy grumbled and rubbed at a leg that had gone to sleep. "Why wouldn't it work this time? It unshrunk the Buckle house *last* night."

"Never you mind, dearie." Old Sybilla tilted her head wearily back against the office wall. "Leastwise, he still don't know about us yet, an' he thinks you two are long gone."

Mr. Crump patted his wife's shoulder. "That's right, old girl. We'll mebbe have another go at it when we get where we're goin' to."

"Where do you s'pose we're *going?*" In a small voice Mindy rephrased her question. But as the questions were really unanswerable, there was no response this time either. Mrs. Morrissey nodded and snored in old Banker Dopple's overstuffed leather armchair, Augustus Dopple dozed fitfully, and the others tried to nap in their corners. Even Mrs. Bright was subdued. Her head bobbed in time with the truck's jiggling, and it was not long before she, too, was mumbling in an uneasy dream.

Mindy unfolded one leg from beneath herself and tucked the other one under her. The prickles of the sleepy leg were so fierce that she had to ease the knee straight, holding her leg by the ankle to steady it. "Oh, if only it had worked!" she whispered to the darkened room. The old people had just begun to get over *their* prickles after so many years of sitting tight, and already they were slipping back into their accustomed lethargy.

The last twinge faded, and Mindy pushed away from the wall, pulling herself up with the aid of a tall hat rack that stood nearby. The bank's jiggle had worsened noticeably, so that both Mindy and the hat rack teetered dangerously. A short dash to the roll-top desk opposite provided a surer support while Mindy cast about in her mind for something to do. *Anything* to do. Anything would be better than sitting like a bump on the baseboard. The bank bucked slightly. Every fourth or fifth jiggle was now followed by a decided jolt that clicked Mindy's teeth together. It was easier, she found, to copy the dozing oldsters and breathe through her mouth rather than her nose. The jarring sensation was twice as noticeable if you set your teeth against it. She moved quietly to the door.

The hallway was as dark as the manager's office, even though the door into the teller's cage in the front room had been propped open. It took some time for Mindy to grope her unsteady way out and up the stairs to the second-floor front office where a circular iron staircase led up into the cupola's cubbyhole of a room.

It was not so dark outside as she had supposed. The long summer evening was just wearing toward its end. She could see that the bank had been hurriedly jammed in on top of a large crate, apparently the one in which they had seen the Professor stow the Emporium. Beyond the window on the left loomed the dark bulk of the Reducer. On the floor below, the windows at the front and on the right-hand side had for view only the battered planks that formed the sides and tailgate of the truck. But here in the cupola, Mindy could see the cloud of dust beyond the tailgate and dark ranks of giant trees crowding up to the rutted road to stretch their arms across it, as if to hide the speeding truck from the evening sky.

"Oof! Glory, this must be what it's like to ride out a storm in a ship's crow's nest!" A grinning Samantha came up the last four steps on her hands and knees. "Any sign of land?"

Mindy left off chewing at a ragged fingernail. "Aye, cap'n, sir. But whether it's far Cathay or Timbuktu you couldn't tell by me. There aren't stars enough out yet even to guess direction. Except I guess we can't be going over east, or Florida way, because the sky is darkest behind us." She bit nervously at a stubborn hangnail. "Maybe we're heading for California."

Samantha pulled out a handkerchief just in time to stifle a sneeze. "Snmf. No, not California. Not on a pokey dirt road like this. The Professor *ought* to be trying to outrun your Horace, but this is a strange way to . . ." She sneezed again. "Phew! What a road! The police should be able to track the Prof by his dust cloud!"

"And we're slowing down even more," Mindy observed, puzzled.

The trees the bouncing truck passed through grew more straggly and drew back from the road. The dust cloud dwindled, and for the first time the road itself was visible—an overgrown and unused dirt track that showed signs in spots of once having been paved. There were chuckholes as plentiful as polka dots, some a yard across.

"How strange!" Samantha spoke in a wondering whisper.

"How strange wha-at?" The truck gave a bone-jarring bounce, and Mindy, off balance, grabbed for the handle at the bottom of the nearest window sash.

Samantha stared. As the sky opened out above and the road dipped downward, she watched intently the hillslope unrolling behind them. Tumbledown rock walls straggled across the neglected fields. A great old Douglas fir towered beside a windowless and crumbling farmhouse perched halfway down the hill.

"Do you know, dear, I think . . ." Samantha faltered. "I was so small, though. How could I remember?" She knelt by the window, her chin propped in her hands, and frowned at the landscape unwinding in the dusk. "That house . . . they had a Chow dog. Chin-Chin! His name was Chin-Chin."

Mindy's eyes blinked wide. "Dopple? You mean it's Dopple we're coming to? It is, isn't it? Oh, don't you *see*? The Professor must think. . . ." Her mind raced to the answer. "I bet it has to be like the Buckle house! He's bringing the bank back where it came from. If he can't adjust his machine, he *can* adjust the place! It must unshrink . . ."

"It must *unshrink* a thing only under the same conditions it first *shrunk* it," Samantha finished excitedly.

"Then it is Dopple we're coming to? It *is*, isn't it?"

Samantha did not have to answer. The truck came to a stop beyond a crazily tilted stone road marker. In the gathering darkness it was just possible to make out the words carved on its sides.

High Street, read one side.

Grace Street, said the other.

Around and beyond were only weedy, empty fields overgrown in patches with elderberries and brambles.

The Professor let down the tailgate.

"Oh dear!" Samantha exclaimed. She turned to Mindy and said in an excited whisper, "Mindy, you must run downstairs as quick as ever you can and tell the old dears what's up. If the Professor is right and the machine can only work on the Dopple houses *in* Dopple, our ambush is on again! Do hurry!" As Mindy swung down the stair, Samantha hissed after her, "I'll come down to the second floor, and the minute we're unshrunk, I'll signal somehow. Whatever you do, keep away from the ground-floor windows."

"OK." Mindy's faint whisper floated upward.

At that moment the bank gave a mighty lurch. Samantha clung for dear life to the iron railing. At the bottom of the circular stair, Mindy was sent slithering out into the dusty hallway on her stomach and came to rest by an office door that bore the legend, DR. B. B. CRUSPIN, D.D.S.—PAINLESS EXTRACTIONS. At least, she thought thankfully, she had been off the iron staircase when the Professor picked up the bank, or she might have been pitched on her head. And that would have been that. She pulled herself up and dusted herself off, keeping one hand firmly on the doorknob. Two would have been better. The bank gave a lesser jolt and settled into a regular stomach-lurching bucking, as if the Professor held it against his thighs as he walked, staggering a little with the weight. His arms covered the windows at each end of the hall, shutting out the waning light. Mindy began to fear she would not reach the others in time. In the next brief lull she ran, groping for the head of the stairway, and reached it to wrap her arms around the newel post beside the top step just in the nick of time. In the next—never letting go of the banister for a moment—she almost gained the landing below, and in another three or four lurches was safely in the downstairs hall.

The manager's office was a shambles. After the first upheaval the elderly adventurers had quite sensibly dashed for the windows, since the handles at the bottoms of the window sashes were the only stationary things in the room. Everything else was on the move. Rolltop desk, tall wooden filing cabinets, overstuffed leather armchair, hat rack, and spittoon rolled merrily from side to side with a great clang and clatter and creaking of casters, and the room's frightened occupants crouched as low as possible below the windowsills for fear the Professor should see them. At the same time, the old gentlemen were much exercised to fend off the careening furniture. It was little to be wondered at, therefore, that when Mindy appeared in the doorway, panting, "The ambush is on again!", they all looked a trifle wild-eyed.

Just then the bank was set down with such a jarring thump that everyone in the bank manager's office, however unwilling, sat down on the floor with an echoing bump.

"Oof!" gasped Herman Goff, red-faced and staring blankly.

"Lawks 'a mussy, it's the end of the world!" wailed Sybilla softly.

"Oh, surely not," ventured the Reverend faintly.

Miss Britomart turned her face to the wall and indulged in a moment of quiet hysterics, while Mrs. Bright murmured sympathetic, soothing little clucks. Nurse Morrissey, with the help of the gentlemen, heaved herself up and went to take a look at Jack Crump's tongue, which he had given a very painful bite when caught unawares by the first jolt.

They heard the sound of an engine and the shifting of gears.

"The vault!" Mindy scrambled to her feet. "We've got to *hurry*. The Professor's brought us to Dopple. We're in Dopple for *real*. Samantha thinks that if he's set us down on the old bank foundations, the Reducer *will* work. We'll be unshrunk, and the Professor could be walking in any minute!"

Augustus Dopple was first to grasp the situation.

The Professor was at that very moment maneuvering the truck into position so that his Reducer pointed at the little bank. Further, Mr. Dopple saw that in his companions' present state, explanations could take an endless while. He held up a hand and said, "Stop!"

Miss Brit stopped fussing with her long silver-blond hair she had been trying to fumble back into a neat coronet. Sybilla left off trying to straighten up the furniture.

"There is no time for thoughts of appearances, ladies," Augustus said sternly. "To your posts!"

"Yes, *sir!*" said Herman Goff, fired with a sudden youthful excitement, like the horse who smells the young green grass after a long, cramped winter shut up in a barn. He shouldered masterfully past the filing cabinets and through the door, narrowly missing Samantha, who stuck her head in briefly with a whispered shriek of *"We're unshrunk!"* and then galloped down the moonlit hall and into her hiding place in the teller's cage.

In a moment Mindy was in place in the outer vault room, across the hall from the door into the teller's cage, crouched ready between a tall file cabinet and the door, which opened inward, hiding her from view. Mrs. Bright slipped into the cloakroom under the steps, and the other ladies tiptoed in a rush into the ladies' washroom. That now rather crowded chamber was next door to the vault room. The gentlemen were divided between the gentlemen's washroom, a stuffy little broom closet, and a large metal safe-cupboard in the outer vault room, from which the shelves had been removed earlier in the day. Because this post was situated in a position of great risk near the vault itself, Augustus Dopple, being sensible of his responsibility to the bank's depositors, had insisted that it must be his. Armed with a neat little blackjack—twenty-five silver dollars tied up in one of his socks—and trembling lest he should have to use it, he waited with an ear to the metal door.

Mindy in her dark corner stared fixedly at the crack of dim light from the hall, as if the wider open her eyes were, the better she could hear.

There was a rattling at the front door.

No one breathed.

The door creaked open, and the sweet smell of night washed through the musty air.

"Ho, ho, anybody home?" chortled a strange voice. "No? Well, that being the case, I reckon I'll just have to help myself, now won't I?"

The ladies in the washroom stared toward each other in the darkness. Who was *that?* Not the Professor! And then Miss Brit remembered that they were unshrunk. The low, rumbling voice they knew as the Professor's when they had been only five-inches-and-a-bit tall was really this wispy little cackle! She suppressed a giggle of delight and reached across the sink to give Sybilla's hand a reassuring pat.

Samantha, in the teller's cage, was the first to see that Kurtz had a bright-beamed searchlight battery lantern. Its brilliant circle of light bounced over the walls and ceiling. She crossed her fingers. As soon as he moved past and through the outer door to the hall, she nipped through the little door at the end of the counter and cut off his retreat by locking the street door behind him.

As the footsteps moved into the hallway, Mindy shrank back in her corner. The light bounced along the doors. There was a pause, and then it speared straight through the outer vault room and lingered on the heavy steel door with its long handle and impressive combination lock.

"Aha! There you are, me proud beauty!" The Professor chuckled at his little witticism as he trotted toward the vault. Setting the lantern down with a clatter, he rubbed his hands together in delight.

The suspense of the next few moments was almost as dreadful for Mindy, who could see, as for the others, who could only strain to hear through their respective doors and walls. It seemed to take years. In a growing ill temper the Professor searched for the combination in desk drawers, among notebooks and files, and even among the ancient jottings on the dusty desk blotter, before the beam of his lantern glanced across the bulletin board on the wall beside the vault and drew him to a neatly printed card that read: *R 23—L 17—R 9.*

It seemed ages more before the Professor's nervous, twitching fingers managed to get the numbers exactly right as he twiddled at the dial, eyes shining, an ear cocked for the telltale click. At last he straightened, pulled down on the long handle with both hands, and swung the vault door open. Mindy eased her door away from the file cabinet.

"Open Sesame!" The chortle was almost a cackle.

Snatching up the lantern, the untidy, wild little old man—so unlike the dapper L. L. Putt of only the day before—rushed into the vault and began pulling at drawers, riffling among the papers, and showering banknotes on the floor with wild abandon. Then he saw the safe-deposit boxes and the drawer labeled UMSTOTT. A key stood in the lock, and dangling from it at the other end of a bit of string was the second key.

He never heard a thing.

Mindy slipped across the room. She gave the steel door a great push, and it clicked shut even before Mr. Dopple unfolded himself from the cupboard.

"Close Sesame," Mindy said faintly. And then something went wrong with her knees, and she sat down on the floor very suddenly.

Dopple had never, even in its youngest days, seen such excitement as in the few hours that followed. The Professor's machine proved quite simple to work. Once a house was in place and the Reducer's snout pointed at it, all that was required was to turn the main switch from *Off* to *Magnify*. One by one the miniature houses (except, of course, the Buckle house, which belonged in Brittlesdale) were placed on their old foundations and restored to their proper proportions with cheers and exclamations of awe. At midnight two State Police cars, a squad car each from Summit, Bedford, and Somerset counties, Officer Beagle in the Brittlesdale car with Mr. and Mrs. Hallam, a Volkswagen full of newspaper reporters, and a shambling, bleary-eyed Horace crept

down the long hill at four miles an hour and pulled to a hesitant stop at the edge of a town that had no business being there. Lights winked cheerfully in the darkness. A church organ could be heard descanting above the notes of frogs and crickets, and somewhere the uneven strains of "The Herd Girl's Dream" tinkled out from a hand-cranked Victrola.

"Goshamighty! I haven't heard that kind of music since my granny's picnic suppers in the old orchard," marveled Officer Beagle. He chuckled. "I used to crank the Sousa marches up tight as the gramaphone'd go, and us kids'd march around till it wound down to a groan and we couldn't march any slower."

In the first state car a captain snapped impatiently, "We've lost track of our turnings. Where's the map? And where has that fool dog gotten to?"

Horace, footsore and as dog-tired as a dog can be, was bewildered at the confused crisscrossing of scents at the first intersection and had begun to wander aimlessly. Then coming upon an empty truck, he suddenly caught the scent he had lost and gave a bark, deep and loud. The searchers stopped talking to listen as Horace barked again. After a second's silence the Dopple church bell gave tongue, pealing out across the hills in answer. The rescuers climbed out of their cars and milled about in the road, shouting back and forth, "Where are we?" and "What's up?" in the darkness, and "What idiot was supposed to be watching the map?" Then they all saw a small figure carrying an old-fashioned bull's-eye lantern come running across the ragged green like a firefly in the waist-high grass.

"Oh, *wait* till I tell you what all *happened*," panted Mindy as she flew into her father's arms.

Fourteen

"I felt all thumpy inside and shivery out, like Gretel pushing the old witch in the oven, I guess." Mindy took another cupcake and carefully peeled away the pleated paper cup. A week had passed, and it was her birthday, and the lunch Miss Brit and Samantha had provided as a birthday-and-all's-well-that-ends-well party was one good thing after another. The little cakes were iced in white, with golden yellow icing roses on top, and instead of ice cream there was sherbet that was a rainbow of colors in each dish.

"It was very brave of Mindy. We were all *quite* terrified." Mrs. Bright beamed at Mr. and Mrs. Hallam, who had already heard the story from Mindy a dozen times in the past week and still marveled at it. "There we all were," Mrs. Bright went on, "afraid to stir for fear young Willie would hear a floorboard creak. Perfectly *frantic* he must have been, putting the bank down as roughly as he did. And then the shock of finding himself caught! It's no wonder he went into a nervous delirium."

Miss Britomart nodded shyly to the Hallams. "At first we feared you might not find us. In the excitement of setting Dopple right again—seeing our houses become themselves again—we *quite* forgot how difficult explaining to the authorities and all those newsmen would be."

Mr. Goff laughed and patted his new silk waistcoat contentedly. "Good thing we had the hang of the way the Prof's machine worked. Nobody'd have believed a word of it otherwise. If you could've seen your faces!" He chuckled, but then sobered. "Mebbe you can tell us, Mr. Hallam. What news is there of Kurtz?"

Mr. Hallam frowned. "Beagle tells me the poor old fellow's completely collapsed. Mad as a hatter. Mammoth Business Machines wants to buy the Reducer and perfect it, but your Professor has gotten it in his head they mean to steal it. He says he won't 'sign any papers,' but of course he can't sign them anyway. He isn't legally responsible in the condition he's in at the moment. Of course, the court will step in and act for him with MBM if he's truly out of his head. If he ever comes out of the hospital, I suppose he'd have a comfortable income from royalties on the invention, but then he'd be liable for criminal prosecution for kidnapping, housenapping, whathave-you. I doubt whether he could face that. He's aged considerably, Beagle says. You needn't worry about his ever getting the Reducer back. *That* I'm sure of." He nodded reassuringly to the oldsters gathered around the festive table.

"*You're* the amazing ones," Mrs. Hallam put in wonderingly, indicating the cheerful new poppy wallpaper and the pleasant view from Miss Umstott's front windows across the green to the church. "A week ago Dopple was up to its eyebrows in a jungle of weeds and scrubby thickets, and now it is all velvety grass and streetlamps and roses and hydrangeas!"

"With plumbing and electricity," added Augustus Dopple with a precise nod and a smile of great contentment.

"*And* wall heaters." Mr. Goff thrust his thumbs in his waistcoat pockets. "Efficient little gizmos. Beats shoveling coal into a furnace all hollow."

Miss Britomart passed a heaping plate of almond brownies. "It was most fascinating," she said, "to watch the young men putting the grass on the green. The sod came in large rolls, and they fitted it for all the world like a carpet. *Most* interesting."

"All thanks to you, Miss Britomart," said Mrs. Morrissey, filling the teacups all around.

"That's right." Mr. Goff beamed. "*New* Dopple's going to be a real showplace, and no mistake. Miss Brit here has done real handsome by us all. Gus worked it all out businesswise, so we've got us a New Dopple Foundation now, set up with all that Mammoth Business Machines stock they got for them Indelible shares. The money'll take care of the place and help make up for Dopple's lost time, you might say."

"I wanted it to be share and share alike," Miss Britt said shyly. "Just as it's been all these years. Then, too, there were so many people who had lost everything when Dopple was whisked away. We hope they will want to return—or that their children and grandchildren may wish to come." Mr. and Mrs. Crump, in fact, she explained, had already set off in a new red station wagon to visit the families of former residents to invite them to return to their old homes, which were being made ready.

"*And,*" said Samantha with a laugh, looking very pretty in a curly hairdo and a bright flowered dress, "we have dozens and dozens of sightseers! Just like the old museum days. One little man wanted to organize us and the New Dopple Foundation into YES-TERDAY, U.S.A.—'The Turn of the Century Town'!"

"Tell 'em what you said to that, Miss Brit!" Mrs. Morrissey chuckled and helped herself to a fourth chocolate eclair.

Miss Britomart dimpled and brushed an imaginary bit of lint from her new silk suit. She smiled charmingly. "I simply said that it would never do. We shall have children here when our old friends and nieces and nephews come, and we *could* not ask children to live in Yesterday! Most especially as *we* have been having such adventures discovering Today." She turned to Mrs. Bright. "Perhaps, Mary, we could persuade the Hallams to come to New Dopple, too? There is the Morley house . . ."

Mindy looked up, dismayed, from a half-eaten cupcake. "Mrs. Bright! Aren't you coming back to Brittlesdale?"

Mrs. Bright's eyebrows went up in a perplexed frown. "I can't decide. I should be very conspicuous if the dear old Buckle house were restored to its old place and size in Brittlesdale. You know how it would be with the highway at my front door! My house and I should be a curiosity. Of course, the house must stay a 'dollhouse' if it remains here; but if ever the Reducer *were* perfected so that it could enlarge objects no matter what their location, it would be quite at home in Dopple. And these dear people are tempting me with a lovely apartment they've fixed up on the upstairs floor of the bank. I am very tempted to stay with our new friends." She twinkled mischievously, her apple-red cheeks glowing. "Yes, we must let your parents see the Morley house. It would make a splendid antique shop."

"Seventeen ninety-eight. Second oldest house in Dopple." Old Augustus Dopple rubbed his hands in a businesslike way as he turned to Mr. Hallam. "The bank owns it. No Morleys left, you see. We would be prepared to offer you very generous terms indeed . . ."

"*Dear* Augustus!" Miss Britomart objected. "You gentlemen must save such talk for another time. We are quite forgetting that we are a birthday party."

After a whispered conference with Miss Britomart and Mrs. Bright, the Reverend and Mr. Goff disappeared from the room. The ladies cleared a space on the table, and in a moment the Reverend had reappeared to the general accompaniment of "Happy Birthday," beaming like a cherub under his halo of soft white hair. On a silver tray he carried a splendid cake—three tiers smothered in white icing, ribbons, and rosettes, with yellow sugar daisies and *Mindy* tastefully written on top in letters made to look like a leafy green vine.

Mindy's eyes shone, but as the oldsters came to the end of the birthday song, her glance fell on the neat little pile of cupcake papers on her plate. Everyone laughed at her distress.

"Don't you fret yourself, dearie." Mrs. Morrissey chuckled, shaking like a large pudding. "The big one's to take home. I reckon you'll find friends enough to help you eat it. It's dear old Sybilla's doing. A sorry-I-couldn't-be-here present, you might say."

Explanation was cut short by Mr. Goff's entrance. "Surprise!" he boomed. He bore a large white box, tied with a yellow lace ribbon, and set it in front of Mindy, letting it down carefully, as if it were very heavy.

"Oh, Mindy, open it quickly!" exclaimed her mother. "And save the ribbon. It's lovely."

Miss Britomart smiled mysteriously as Mindy worked to slide the ribbon off. "This was mine when I was your age, Araminta," she said. "And it was my mother's before that. It was the best 'thank you' we could think of. *And* the best 'reminder,' so that you may not forget us."

As the lacy bow pulled free, the sides of the box

fell outward to reveal a lovely old dollhouse, freshly painted and refurbished. Taped to one chimney was a small card, which announced in spidery handwriting: GUARANTEED UNSHRUNK.